About the author

G.M. Savage has always been inspired by nature, and his writing is no different. He enjoyed classics like *Where the Red Fern Grows* and *Hatchet* growing up but didn't know he wanted to become a writer until reading *A River Runs Through It* in college. Mr. Savage aims to take readers to uncharted landscapes through his stories. He encourages young readers to go on an outdoor adventure, even if it's only to the backyard.

When he's not writing, G.M. Savage enjoys spending time with family and friends. He also enjoys fly-fishing, hiking, and mountain biking in the Pocono Mountains of Pennsylvania. You can connect with G.M. Savage via his website: www.gmsavage.org

JACK MATHIAS AND THE BOONETOWN BANDITS

G.M. Savage

JACK MATHIAS AND THE BOONETOWN BANDITS

Vanguard Press

VANGUARD PAPERBACK

© Copyright 2022
G.M. Savage

A CIP catalogue record for this title is
available from the British Library.

ISBN 978 1 80016 254 9

*Vanguard Press is an imprint of
Pegasus Elliot MacKenzie Publishers Ltd.*
www.pegasuspublishers.com

First Published in 2022

**Vanguard Press
Sheraton House Castle Park
Cambridge England**

Printed & Bound in Great Britain

Prologue

In Boonetown, there were two unarguable truths.

The first: after you passed the brick clock tower in the town square and crossed the red covered bridge that stretched over the Gauley River, you'd find—nestled between the pines and sycamores—Boonetown Middle School.

The second, and often more obvious, truth: if there was trouble, surely Jack Mathias was the cause.

Chapter 1
The Prank

Boonetown Middle School

10:58 a.m. Boonetown Middle School

"This is going to be awesome," Jack said under his breath, as he hovered over the water fountain and rolled a wet paper ball between his fingertips. Jack wiggled and twisted his newly constructed spitball deep into the fountain's tap. He looked left and right down the seventh-grade hallway. He had time. Jack pulled a maple syrup packet from his pocket—God bless the cafeteria—bit into it, and squirted the syrup into the crevices around the water fountain's push button.

"Tim, check this out," Jack said, elbowing Tim, his seventh-grade classmate and accomplice in most, if not all, pranks. "When Gene gets a drink, it'll shoot his glasses off! Might even shoot up his nose!"

They shared a laugh. Gene was Jack's next-door neighbor, and an easy target for pranks.

"You can't seem to give this boy a break, Jack," Tim said, laughing.

"Ahh, it's all in fun. He'll laugh it off as long as his book doesn't get wet. And it's payback. He tells my parents everything," Jack said, inspecting his masterwork with bright eyes—it was perfect.

"I see him coming." Tim pointed down the hallway. "Come on, let's go!"

Jack and Tim darted into the boys' room, just feet away, and peered around the corner and watched Gene approach. Gene's face was buried in a book, as always, and he walked with the school-known slouch, also known to some as "Gene Slouch."

Gene always stopped to take a sip from the water fountain as if he was compelled to do it whenever he saw one. He lowered his book and walked to the fountain.

Jack could barely contain himself. His dimples were on full display. His plan was going smoother than any other. Gene leaned to take a sip. Jack held his breath the entire time. Here was the good part.

"Gene!" A voice came from the entryway of the women's bathroom. "I've been looking for you."

Gene stopped. Jack's grin vanished. This was the one voice he didn't want to hear. Not now.

"Oh, no," Jack whispered. "This is not good!"

"Mrs. Bombgardner," Gene said with a soft bow.

"Did you finish the book you borrowed last week?" Mrs. Bombgardner asked with a light, raspy tone.

She stood next to Gene, adjusting her thick glasses with a gleeful smile. Gene was her favorite, her most frequent customer in the school's library. Of course, she had to stop and say hello.

"I'm on the last chapter. I'll return it tomorrow!" Gene showed her the book and put out his hands, pointing at the fountain. "Ladies first."

"She doesn't want a drink. She doesn't deserve this, you idiot," Jack muttered. "Can't you be rude for once, Gene?"

"Aren't you such a gentleman!" Mrs. Bombgardner said and leaned forward. "You'd be a scholar at Hogwarts school."

They shared a laugh, in tune with each other, and Mrs. Bombgardner turned to the fountain.

"No…" Jack pressed his back against the bathroom wall and covered his eyes.

"Aaiie!" A shrill pierced down the hallway, and a shrill had never been louder or more terrifying.

Water torrented on Mrs. Bombgardner's face. The continuous stream of water shot like a missile into her glasses and up her nostrils for what seemed like an eternity.

Why did this prank have to be so good? Why now?

Dozens of footsteps ran closer, yelling a barrage of questions like "What happened?" "Is it a fire drill?" and "Did Steve 'Squeaker' McShartski's gas turn to liquid again," among many others in the noisy chaos.

But the questions quickly turned to laughter when they witnessed Mrs. Bombgardner.

"Stop laughing!" Mrs. Bombgardner yelled.

The students laughed harder while Mrs. Bombgardner grew louder. Jack turned around to come up with a plan, but he only witnessed Tim's feet exiting out of the bathroom window. *Oh, great!* Jack thought.

Jack screwed up. No, Gene screwed everything up: Gene and his over-the-top kindness when it came to adults. Jack was running out of options. If he remained hidden, they would all know it was him. They already suspected him probably. But there was another option.

Jack bolted out of the bathroom and tried to keep a straight face at the hilarious sight.

Mrs. Bombgardner's permed, bouffant hair was soaked, and her glasses knocked to the side. She wheezed slowly, in rage.

Jack tried to act surprised, his mouth a big O of disbelief.

"Gene!" Jack shouted. "What the heck did you do?"

"I didn't do anything!" Gene yelled, desperately looking around for a place to hide.

Water dripped off Mrs. Bombgardner's portly face onto her soaked white blouse as she opened her mouth and closed it again. Her eye twitched.

"This is some serious bad luck, Mrs. Bombgardner," Jack said, inspecting the water fountain. "There must be something wrong with it."

Mrs. Bombgardner was about to speak, but no words came out of her mouth. Her eyes were wide and her jaw trembling. She might have wanted to scold them, but Mrs. Bombgardner didn't seem able to process things properly.

She turned down the hallway and slipped on the pooling fountain water, falling back into the puddle. Water splashed everywhere.

The laughter resumed, louder this time, surrounding Mrs. Bombgardner like a hurricane as she tried to get on her feet.

"Let me help you," Jack said, offering his hand.

"Stay away, I'm fine!" she yelled, getting back to her feet.

She staggered down the hallway, her orthopedic shoes squeaking with each trembling step.

She glared at each student she passed by. Her left hand clenched her wet shirt as she tried to wring it out.

"Go back to class, you hear?" Mrs. Bombgardner yelled, before she pulled open and slammed the office door.

Down the hallway, Jack and Gene looked around at the aftermath. Jack placed his hand on Gene's shoulder.

"Whoa, Gene, even I wouldn't pull such a prank on Mrs. Bombgardner," Jack said, raising his eyebrows.

"Really?" Gene shot Jack a look through his black-framed glasses.

Chapter 2
Call to the Office

One Week Later

The third-period bell rang as the cheery children of Boonetown Middle School shuffled to their rooms. Flip flops, t-shirts, and shorts dominated the fashion trend since summer vacation was only a few short days away. On these days, you could find lines of students outside the office, waiting to have their shorts measured by the fingertip test. Students who failed this test were rewarded with a nice, clean pair of class of '96 sweatpants, or even worse, grandpa slacks with suspenders. Fancy!

Meanwhile, in the West Wing of the school, Mr. Bowman's class—the one that usually smelled of sloppy joes, glue, and sawdust—took on a different smell this time of year. One of fresh cut grass and coconut oil. It was a changeup that many students welcomed from the overall giddiness of the room—except for the allergy-prone students, who hovered over the trash can and fired away snot rockets.

In the fourth row, Jack Mathias sat in his seat, carving—with a pencil—into his big eraser. As he finished the initials JM, his classmate Casey Jones approached him.

"Here you go," Casey whispered, holding out a folded note.

Jack looked at the note with the first letter of the name covered by Casey's pink thumbnail.

"From: a-r-a-h. Sarah!" Jack read, before he dropped his pencil and shot his arm out. "Thank you." Jack grabbed and feverishly opened the note.

Jack, who was usually too enamored with his own thoughts and personal conquests, showed a side few had seen. He clung to the letter with both hands, and took a deep breath, and then another. "Oh, my god, oh, my god, Sarah's finally going to say she loves me," Jack said under his breath.

Jack read:

Dear Jack,
You made me laugh all year, I'm not sure if you noticed me, or feel the same way.

Jack put the note down and looked up to the ceiling as a big smile appeared. "You have no idea! Thank you! Thank you!" he said, shaking his fists, before reading on.

I thought it was funny how you would make Mrs. Splat so mad in art, with your hybrid man/chupacabra/fox finger paintings. I knew it was supposed to be a big, fluffy tail, despite what everyone

15

else thought. If it wasn't, it's okay. Even when you do horribly bad things, there's something in your smile, the shine of your hair, and the gaze in your eyes that makes me trust you, no matter what! It feels comforting.

"She's so feelin' me," Jack said, nodding his head while running his hand through his thick hair.

Anyway, I wrote you a rhyme. Don't laugh.
In three more days, it will be summer,
but in three more days,
it will be a bummer if I don't c. u.

"Wait, what?" Jack's head jolted back as he squinted. "That's pretty lame coming from Sarah, the poetry queen."

I don't want to be a fool, but would you like to hang with me at the pool, just U.N.I. next week?
Love,
Tarah

"Wait, Tarah, not Sarah?" Jack rubbed his eyes and looked again. "Tarah, in the front row, who snorts when she laughs? Oh, my god!" Jack looked up to see Tarah winking at him, with her pink pigtails sticking up. Jack slammed the letter down and slumped in his seat.

Ten minutes into class, it was clear that Mr. Bowman had already started his summer vacation and packed it in for the year. He handed out travel brochures of *The Rivers and Streams of the Boonetown Valley*. Jack's brochure was put to good use. It lay punctured on his desk, serving as the base of his control tower; it was constructed of twelve and a half No. 2 pencils, each connected from pencil point to eraser, and towering several feet above his desk. Jack then crafted the note he received from Tarah into a paper airplane. He noticed the scowl on her face when she glanced back. After making the final fold and creasing it, Jack admired the astral plane from end to end with the attention of a kid that plans to one day become an aerospace engineer. He was not making a simple paper plane; he may as well have been crafting a rocket to the moon. The grin on his face and the pride in his eyes showed how much he enjoyed it.

Finished with his plane, he held it up proudly. He turned in his seat to two students who sat beside him.

"Hey, guys," Jack said, cupping his mouth like a megaphone while holding the plane. "This is air traffic control. We got an erect rocket heading for the seventh planet. It's coming in hot. Code brown, code brown!"

But before they could react, the classroom telephone buzzed, and it caught Jack's attention. Everyone looked in Jack's direction. More often than not, the call was from Principal Kinsey summoning Jack to his office.

Mr. Bowman answered the phone and moments later said, "Of course." He looked at the class before he covered the phone and whispered, "You know he was the ringleader to that Mr. Butt-man stuff earlier in the year. I just found out. Yeah, I know, just a few more days. Okay, bye." Mr. Bowman nodded and hung up the phone. "Jack!"

"Ooohh." The class roared with laughter.

"Quiet down," Mr. Bowman said. He barely looked in Jack's direction and hitched his thumb toward the door. "Hit it, Jack. You know the drill."

"I'm free," he shouted.

Jack stood up, and the tower of pencils collapsed and scattered about the floor. Before he left the room, he launched the paper airplane toward Mr. Bowman's desk. The plane somehow managed to take an entire loop around the room before it settled into a wide arc, lowering itself and landing in Mr. Bowman's wild hair.

He was rewarded by another sweeping "Wooh" from the class. Some even applauded, and it was those sounds of encouragement that seemed to push him out the door, headed to the principal's office for what he believed might be the thirtieth time this year.

Jack shuffled down the hallway; his sneakers squeaked on the polished floors. He didn't really mind going to Principal Kinsey's office. He didn't exactly like it either. He was a bit confused.

Why would I get called down on the last week of school? Jack thought. *Kinsey usually lets things go. Whatever. As long as I don't miss summer camp, I'm good.*

On the bright side, at least he got to leave class and walk around the school for a bit. Before leaving the seventh-grade hallway, he darted to his locker to put on his hoodie. For whatever reason, this gave him comfort when sitting across from Principal Kinsey.

As Jack rounded the corner from his locker, he saw something bright approaching—a moving and shining light coming right at him.

"Oh, my god, it's her."

Chapter 3
All Halls Lead to Doom

Jack froze in the middle of the hallway. His stomach felt like it had gone over the first crest on a roller coaster and taken the steep plunge. Jack's mind looped, and his heart raced. It was Sarah Sharp. Sarah was the one girl Jack had any real interest in, but as luck would have it, she was one of the few that seemed to not care much about him at all.

He smiled but then his mouth opened, and words spilled out—words he was not sure of but was helpless to stop. "H-Hey, Sarah."

Sarah nodded and smiled back. He could not tell if she was merely being polite or if she was actually happy to see him. Sarah was so hard to read. She was the student council president and was heavily involved in planning all of the parties and dances at the school. Sarah had long flowing brunette hair that resembled the finest silk money could buy, and her blue eyes reminded him of the country club swimming pool, where he went to swim with his cousin—when he wasn't grounded.

The simplest things like talking seemed hard when he was around her. His mind seemed to shut down, and his mouth just flapped up and down, uttering useless, stupid words. Worst of all, he could not seem to take his eyes off her whenever she was within speaking distance. And the memories of the fifth-grade roller skating party still haunted him, two years later. He won the limbo, fastest skater, and even won a stuffed animal for her that day. He couldn't have been any more perfect. But when he asked her out, her lips opened, she let out a breath, and the letters inside of that breath were, N-O, No. Ouch!

"Hey, Jack," she said without stopping.

"So, hey, guess where I'm headed?"

"The principal's office, no doubt—again. You must be so proud."

"Yeah... I... Um..."

But Sarah had already walked past him, shaking her head and looking down the hallway.

"See you later," he called out to her. "You know you love me."

"I assure you, I do not," Sarah said, as the sound of her shoes on the floor dissipated in the distance.

Jack watched her turn the corner. His shoulders sagged. He wasn't sure why he was so hung up on Sarah. Maybe it was because he knew she was out of reach. Maybe that was why he liked her so much. Something about reaching for the impossible.

He shrugged and continued on to the office, feeling a little less joyful than he had when he left Mr. Bowman's class. He even noticed his hoodie felt a little heavier than normal also. It must have been the Sarah effect. Jack trudged on, and a familiar face appeared from around the corner.

"Hey, Gene," Jack said.

"Hey, what are you doing, other than obviously scaring Sarah away?" Gene said.

"Whatever, Gene."

Growing up beside each other, Jack and Gene had known each other since they could crawl. While they spent ample time together outside of school, they rarely hung out inside of school. They were an unlikely duo. Jack was popular and the only subject he excelled in was P.E. Gene, on the other hand, was a permanent fixture on the office bulletin board for being labeled "Boonetown's Brightest." A feat Jack didn't envy. Their approach to life differed also. Jack saw the world as his own personal theme park—only a colossal theme park, with roller coasters that broke the sound barrier, and tilt-a-whirls that made the weak vomit uncontrollably for hours after the ride was over. *Blaargh*

Jack knew he was tougher than most, a true warrior. While Gene was a worrier at heart. He always looked at the world through his big glasses like he did not trust it—not his peers, not the ground, not even the sky. He always had a look on his face like he was expecting something bad to happen at any moment. Regardless, Jack in private considered Gene his best friend, and Gene over the years began to warm up to the idea.

"I was just saying," Gene said.

"Where are you headed anyway?" Jack asked. "The library, I bet. Nerd."

It was a safe bet, and both Jack and Gene knew it. Gene's passion for reading rivaled Jack's passion for… well, for Jack and anything he might consider an adventure.

"Just came back from the bathroom and heard this awful crashing sound. So, I came to check it out."

"I didn't hear any crashing sound," Jack said. "What was it?"

"I think it was your ego. And your chances of ever getting Sarah to ever go out with you."

Jack waved the comment away. "Get out of here. You'd think all that reading would make you better at insults."

"Oh, I've got plenty more if you want to hear them."

"No, thanks," Jack said with a playful smile. "Oh, hey… you excited for Woodward bike camp?"

"Umm, yeah!" Gene said, as his face lit up and his shoulders lifted.

"Yeah! I've been counting the days since like September for it." Jack's face beamed. "Only a few more weeks! So, what are you doing this evening?"

"Not sure. Why?"

"Figured we could hang out… maybe take the bikes out, get ready for camp. You know, hit up the track."

"Sounds like a plan. Where are you going now?" Gene asked.

"Kinsey's. I'm guessing because of the Bombgardner incident." Jack shrugged. "But it's all good, the camera doesn't even work, so he has no proof."

"What?" Gene said, pointing at Jack, "You! I knew it! Lies!" Gene shook his head.

Jack smiled back.

"Oh, wait. Come to think of it, no, it's not the Mrs. Bombgardner thing. This is not good, Jack!" Gene's voice raised and his arms shot out spastically. "Principal Kinsey clearly states in the handbook, all infractions unless punished by law, will be dropped within forty-eight hours to make a clear correlation between the behavior and the consequence."

"Wait… so what are you trying to say?" Jack asked.

"Umm, it's the last week of school. So, it's probably about summer school? Maybe no summer camp?" Gene said, hoping Jack would connect the dots.

"Yeah, I doubt it, though, I mean…" Jack was suddenly interrupted by a noise in the distance. Jack looked up the hallway. "Wait, do you hear that, is that who I think it is?

Ba bum bum ba bum bum. Loud high-pitched sounds that resembled a brass instrument playing random off-key notes.

"Yep!" Jack said. "It's Squeaker!"

Steve "Squeaker's" wiry body was clenched tight, and his steps were pigeon-toed. This was a regular occurrence since he had a history of farts gone awry.

Jack cheered and raised his arms. "You can make it, Squeaker! Woo! No grandpa suspenders today!"

Gene laughed and pumped his fists. "Go, Squeaker!"

Squeaker raced through the center of the hallway between Jack and Gene, winced a zit-faced smile, and held a thumb up as he flew past them toward the bathroom. He resembled a power walker—with his arms moving back and forth—except the finish line was a toilet.

"I think he's going to make it today, man!" Jack said, pointing at Squeaker's lower half from down the hall. "You can tell, when his cheeks are squeezed that tight, and his feet cross each other, it's enough to hold usually. He gets in trouble when he does the prance/skip walk."

Gene shook his head and smiled. "Dude, you should put that much attention into studying!"

Squeaker entered the bathroom and let out one last bellowed, tuba-pitched fart. It started strong, amplified by the tile, and then went flat, before tailing off with a dreaded muffled sound.

Squeaker stopped immediately. Nothing more needed to be said when he hunched over, and his hands touched his knees in surrender.

"Oh, man." Jack shook his head, "Well, guess I was wrong."

"Yep!" Gene agreed, before he pointed his index finger from Jack, to Squeaker, and back to Jack again. "Make the connection, Jack. It's a simile: Squeaker's underwear is like your upcoming summer."

Jack swatted Gene's hand away. "Get out! Ugh, God, I hope you're wrong!" Jack said, walking away.

"Yeah, me too," Gene nodded.

Chapter 4
A Fate Worse than Death

Whenever Jack saw the hallway that led to Principal Kinsey's office, he thought of long, cavernous tunnels in some of those old movies he'd seen on TV. The tunnels were usually filled with booby traps, skeletons, and spiders. The only difference was that rather than the dusty floors of some cavern, the hallways of Boonetown Middle School were sparkling and clean.

Jack paused a moment outside the office door. He racked his brain trying to remember what he might have done to precipitate this call to the principal. Other than the incident with Mrs. Bombgardner, Jack's mind was blank. He chuckled to himself. *Can't think of a thing. I'm clean.*

Kinsey's office was a room all its own, separated from the school's central office where lunch menus and school IDs were made. It was also just across from the nurse, another place Jack frequented, usually with a fake stomachache. The entrance to Kinsey's office was nothing more than a set of double doors, a shade of red so dark it might as well be black. There were no windows, not in the doors or the walls, so once you stepped inside, it was easy to feel trapped.

Jack approached the doors and thought about what he might say. He'd tried every trick in the book and nothing seemed to work. Most of the teachers could be fooled by flattery, but Kinsey was something different. He swallowed and scrolled through his emergency list of greetings and comments.

"Nice tie today, Principal Kinsey."

"Whoa, are you working out?"

"Have you lost weight?"

"That was some good sloppy joe at lunch today, huh?"

Nothing ever really worked on him, but Jack was not the kind of kid who gave up easily. He was stubborn and he considered that a character trait to be admired. So, he put on his game face, squared his shoulders, and prepared to face the music. Before he went in, he said his usual good luck prayer.

"Please, God, save me! It wasn't my fault; it was the thoughts in my head. I'm a good—" Jack was interrupted by the opening door. Jack opened his eyes. "God?"

"Jack!" Kinsey motioned with his head to come on in. "I have been compared to many things, but that, my friend, is blasphemy," Principal Kinsey said in his baritone voice, before walking to his throne.

Principal Kinsey was a tall and lean man. He had an aura of seriousness and demanded the best out of staff and students alike. It was almost like he was meant to hold a position of power.

He stared at Jack, still standing in the doorway.

"You know the drill. Come on in and take a seat." Principal Kinsey motioned to the chair.

"Okay…"

There were always two chairs in front of Kinsey's desk. Jack knew the desk wasn't any bigger than the desks his teachers sat behind, but it seemed like a mountain as Jack plopped himself down in one of the chairs. It was a hard plastic chair, the sort that always made his butt hurt if he sat in them long enough. Every time he sat in one of these chairs while in Kinsey's office, he couldn't help but notice the nice and comfortable-looking cushioned chair Kinsey was perched in.

"Nice tie, Mr. Kinsey," Jack said.

No response. The principal just glared at him. Jack swallowed again, hard.

"Good lunch today, sir."

Still nothing.

"I suppose you are wondering why you are here?" Kinsey asked, before he leaned back in his big, comfy chair and locked his fingers behind his head.

"Well, I guess I should be honest with you," Jack said, knowing this was a good first line that Kinsey was a sucker for. "I think it might have something to do with that Mrs. Bombgardner thing. I really am sorry about it, sir. It was just that, well, the joke was meant for someone else. Not a teacher. That's for sure."

"What prank was this now?" Kinsey asked, as he tilted his head and blinked rapidly, almost to the point that his eyelashes resembled a bat flapping its wings.

29

"The water fountain in the seventh-grade hallway…
I wanted to see how the water pressure worked. Sort of
like a science experiment. And yeah, even if it was meant
for a friend, I know it was wrong. But then Mrs.
Bombgardner butted in line, and she was the one that
caught it… Right to the face and all over her dress."

Principal Kinsey unlocked his fingers, ran them
through his finely trimmed mustache, and leaned
forward. "As heinous as that was, Jack, that is not the
reason I called you in here."

"Seriously?" Jack felt his forehead wrinkle. His
brain fired off as many reasons as possible why he could
have been summoned to the office, but nothing stuck.
Well, Gene's summer school theory was a possibility, but
Jack struggled with accepting thoughts that weren't his
own. Especially ideas with unwanted outcomes. Jack
broke from his deep thought and said, "Sorry, sir, but I
don't have a clue."

Just then, a buzzer sounded on Mr. Kinsey's desk
phone. The principal pushed the lit button. "Yes,
Nancy?"

And then what Jack heard next struck fear so
powerful through his chest that he forgot how to breathe
for a moment.

"Miss Crankshaw is here."

*Miss Crankshaw? The guidance counselor? Why?
What could this mean?*

"Ask her to come in," Mr. Kinsey said. He glared at
Jack.

Jack felt his face flush. "Um, sir, why is Miss Crankshaw here?"

Principal Kinsey gave a stern look and tapped some papers on his desk. "I'm certain if you thought hard enough, you'd figure it out, Jack. How was your last report card?"

"Report card?" Jack pushed his hand through his hair. "Not so good, I suppose, but—"

The door opened and Miss Crankshaw entered. She was nice enough, or so Jack thought. A tall woman with curly hair and perfectly round glasses. She doubled as the tennis coach, and as far as Jack was concerned, someone he rarely spoke to.

"Hi, Jack," Miss Crankshaw said. She nodded toward Mr. Kinsey.

"Jack," Mr. Kinsey said, "Miss Crankshaw asked me to be present when she told the bad news. She's already sent an email to your mother."

Jack's heart pounded. His palms poured sweat. His stomach churned like a rolling ocean. He lifted his shoulders and tried to find the Jack charm he could so often rely on, but it failed him today. "Wh-What seems to be the problem?"

Suddenly a low-pitched rumble echoed from Jack's front hoodie pocket. Jack looked down, and Mr. Kinsey and Miss Crankshaw followed suit.

"Um, are you okay, Jack?" Kinsey asked, as his pupils tunneled in on Jack's front hoodie pocket.

Ribbit.

Jack leaned back in his chair and reached into his hoodie pocket.

"Oh, my god, Harley! You're alive!" Jack smiled as he stared at the green blob with blinking eyes, perched in his hand.

Harley—Jack's juvenile bullfrog—leaped from Jack's hand and landed in Principal Kinsey's coffee mug, splattering coffee all over Kinsey's papers, before it hopped onto his desk and around the room.

Principal Kinsey and Miss Crankshaw jumped back, looking on in horror.

"Jack, what is this? You can't bring pets into school!" Kinsey yelled.

"I'm so sorry, I completely forgot. Honestly!" Jack stood up and put his hands out. "I thought my mom flushed him down the toilet, because I couldn't find him this morning!"

Mr. Kinsey ran out of the office and called in Janitor Havens.

Janitor Havens entered the room. He was a thick and burly man, and about thirty years past his athletic prime. However, Havens was still unaware of that. He'd been on Principal Kinsey's radar for quite some time since he took four weeks' paid leave for tearing his rotator cuff while playing dodgeball during work hours with students. Kinsey also didn't appreciate Havens' floor stripper fiasco earlier in the year. But, in Haven's defense, it was an honest misunderstanding caused by a Google search that left out a keyword.

Janitor Havens promptly soaked up the coffee on Kinsey's desk while Jack sat back and watched the unfolding escapades. Principal Kinsey stood up in his nice suit and orchestrated the capture of Harley.

"Let's corner him," Kinsey said.

Principal Kinsey, Miss Crankshaw, and Janitor Havens spread out, arm's length from each other, and forced Harley into the corner of the room. Kinsey took charge.

"Stand back. I'm going in," Kinsey said, as he walked up and towered over Harley. He bent over and picked him up. But all of a sudden…

"Eeeeeeii!" Kinsey made a falsetto scream and dropped Harley. Kinsey flapped his hands and made a ballerina-like pirouette maneuver. "He peed on me!" Kinsey yelled, before running out of the office toward the bathroom. Principal Kinsey could still be heard yelling down the hallway until the bathroom door shut.

Janitor Havens took charge and turned to Miss Crankshaw.

"Stay here, Miss C. I'll get the net," Janitor Havens said in a deep, scratchy voice, before running out of the room.

After several dives, barrel rolls, and lunges, catching only air in the net, Janitor Havens finally succeeded.

"Got ya!" Havens said, latching on to Harley on the floor. "You don't mess with the best."

Janitor Havens clearly either suffered from amnesia or didn't know the meaning of the word "best."

Nonetheless, he carried Harley over to the nurse to stay for the rest of the day.

Minutes later, when all was settled, Kinsey and Miss Crankshaw sat back down, trying to overlook the bullfrog in the room. Kinsey adjusted his tie and said, "Okay, where were we?"

"Oh, yeah," Jack nudged. "Why summer school isn't psychologically good for kids."

"Ha-ha, good one," Kinsey intervened, before motioning to Miss Crankshaw.

"It's your grades," Miss Crankshaw said. "Your teachers tried everything to help you bring them up, and nothing has worked." She looked at Mr. Kinsey. "Especially your history and English grades. You failed."

"And so, Jack," Mr. Kinsey said, "if you expect to get promoted to the next grade, you will need to attend summer school."

Miss Crankshaw smiled toward Jack. "It's the only way. Unless you want to repeat."

Jack looked into Mr. Kinsey's steely gray eyes with the crow's feet jutting out toward his ears. "So, it's not about the water fountain, then?"

Principal Kinsey shook his head.

"No. To be honest with you, we thought it was a malfunction. We sent the janitors down there to fix the fountain because Mrs. Bombgardner thought there was a water pressure issue. She didn't know it was a prank."

34

"Oh." Jack wasn't sure if it was a good or a bad thing that Kinsey didn't seem at all surprised or even really all that upset.

"But now I do know it was a prank." Slowly Principal Kinsey's face turned an odd shade of red. Jack had seen it happen before and knew what was coming: an outburst of the worst kind.

"Do you realize how much wasted energy you caused?" Kinsey asked. "The janitor had to take a perfectly functional water fountain apart, Mrs. Bombgardner had to go home, and we had to send in a temporary sub. All because you—"

Miss Crankshaw cleared her throat. "But that's not the reason we are here today."

Principal Kinsey took a deep breath and closed his eyes. Jack wondered if he was silently counting to ten as he tried to get control of himself. He noted that Kinsey had a tight kung fu grip on the pen he always kept on the edge of his desk.

"Okay, well, that was another issue that will be dealt with at a later date," Kinsey finally said. "As for this visit… Well, Miss Crankshaw told you the hard truth. But what I want to know is why, Jack? You are a bright, smart young man. Your teachers say you hand in homework that is only partially finished, filled with sketches of toilets, hybrid animals, and dinosaurs on them."

Jack could not argue with this because it was absolutely true.

"Jack, we've given you every chance possible. Even let you retake tests as many as three times just so you could get a barely passing grade," Miss Crankshaw said. "But we can't do that any more. Summer school is your only option, and you must pass each class."

Jack cringed at every word. He gasped. "Su… Summer school?" Surely such a punishment was only seen in movies. It would be far too horrific to actually place on some poor kid, right?

Miss Crankshaw nodded.

"And you already emailed my mom?" Jack asked.

"Yes, Jack."

The words "summer school" echoed in Jack's head for a short eternity. Reminiscent of Sarah's "N-O" years earlier. For a moment, Jack was pretty sure he was going to pass out.

"Wait, wait, there must be some mistake," Jack said, in a panic. "There has to be something else. I have Woodward bike camp coming up! This will ruin my life!"

"The only mistake was made by you, Jack," Mr. Kinsey said. "The mistake was the absolute lack of interest and the attitude you've shown all year. So, starting on June 16th, you will be paying for that mistake. That's two weeks, Jack."

"Can't we negotiate? How about, hmm… How about I'll help clean the bathrooms for a day over the summer?"

"No, Jack," Miss Crankshaw said. "I warned you months ago to bring up your grades. You have so much potential."

Jack slumped in the chair. He had heard those words before.

"There's no way out of this now," Miss Crankshaw said. "It's either summer school or you repeat the seventh-grade next year."

"Yeah, you said that. I-I guess I have to—" he gulped more air, "—go to summer school." And in that instant, any great plans Jack had conjured for the summer flew out the window.

Jack had never seen Kinsey so grave and serious before. Angry, sure. Upset, obviously. But never this serious. He knew there was no way out of it. Failing grades trumped some dumb prank.

Jack slumped in his seat. "How long will I have to go for?"

"To make up the grades and get in the appropriate amount of work, it will last until August 20th," Miss Crankshaw said.

"Wait. That means I'll only have a total of nine days of summer vacation."

"See? Math, not so hard, was it?" Principal Kinsey said.

Jack cringed. That was actually a good catch by Kinsey. Ugh.

Kinsey looked at his watch. "All right, Jack. I have other things I must attend to. Any other logistics pertaining to summer school will be in the email we sent to your mom. Miss Crankshaw will call to discuss with your mom as well. Go back to class."

Miss Crankshaw smiled. "We're just looking out for you, Jack. It's for the best."

Jack stood up slowly and walked out of the office. Principal Kinsey followed Jack and shut the door behind him.

"He's a piece of work," Kinsey said, shaking his head and loosening his tie before he sat down. "I can't imagine even one more year with him, much less two!"

"Mr. Kinsey, Jack means well," Miss Crankshaw said. "Even the kids he pranks actually like him and ask for him not to get in trouble."

Kinsey interrupted. "I mean, come on! He steals lunches! He breaks into lockers, plays pranks, and has no respect for authority! I don't care how long it takes, I will push good into him one way or another."

"Well, I looked into all of his offenses, and yes, Jack is to blame, you're right," Miss Crankshaw said in agreement. "But one time—and yes, I know, just one time out of the thirty or so things—but that one time, he was actually stealing lunches to give to the new kid who didn't have much food at home. And he was breaking into his locker to put the food there so nobody knew he did it."

Principal Kinsey scratched his chin. "Well, why didn't he tell anyone that?"

"Because… I don't know. Jack's stubborn and didn't want to be seen as nice?" Miss Crankshaw shook her head and shrugged. "He'd rather get in trouble, I… I guess. I'll admit, he's a tough kid to understand and I don't have the answer. But instead of trying to push the good into him, maybe we can just give him the right environment and be patient and let the good shine through him."

Principal Kinsey's phone rang.

"Let's circle back on this over the summer, okay?" Kinsey said.

Miss Crankshaw nodded and left the room as Principal Kinsey picked up the phone.

"Hello? Wait—what? Steven McShartski did it again? And we don't have any clean pants left? Ugh!"

Chapter 5
Grounded

Jack had never been more thankful for the smell of diesel fumes and warm rubber seats. He smelled these glorious scents as the folding double doors of the bus opened before him. He sat with Gene, but neither of them said much. Somehow word of Jack's terrible news had made it to some of the smaller, less popular circles in the school. He guessed Gene already knew, and that was why he was being so quiet.

Finally, after exactly nineteen minutes (he and Gene had timed it on several occasions), the bus stopped at their street. Many times, Jack compared the feel of stepping back onto non-school property to how Neil Armstrong must have felt when first stepping onto the moon. Jack's feet hit the ground and he let out a sigh of relief as the sound of the school bus engine dissipated down the street.

"You okay?" Gene asked.

"I guess. I'm thinking Woodward's out the window. But hopefully my parents won't be too hard on me. They were probably expecting me to go to summer school."

Gene shuddered. "Oh, don't even say the words 'summer school.' But don't let it twist you up too much," Gene said. "Hey, are we still on for riding tonight?"

"Well, yeah! Besides, my bikes in my room and I can just put that mannequin in my closet under the sheets, so I can sneak out the window."

"Nice. I'll see you then," Gene said, before walking toward his house.

"Later!"

They lived on a quiet street, noisy only on the occasional Saturday when more than one family happened to be having a cookout. On most weekdays, though, it was almost too quiet.

Jack opened the front door of his house, gingerly closed it, and tiptoed in. Any sign of his parents and he was a dead man. He looked down the hallway and saw the coast was clear. Sneaking through the sparsely lit house, he saw only open space to the backdoor, and a clear escape to his tree house. As Jack rounded the corner to the kitchen, he peaked around, and all of a sudden *meeeow…*

Startled, Jack jumped back and looked at his feet. "Morgan, shhhhh!" Jack put his index finger to his mouth and went onto his hands and knees. He crawled across the kitchen floor to the back door, covertly slid the glass door open, and barrel-rolled into the backyard.

"Phew!" Jack exhaled as he lay on his back, before crawling back to close the door.

Knowing the mission was complete, Jack came to his feet, ran to the foot of his tree house, and climbed up the rope to his sacred lair.

The tree house was bare boned. It was mostly constructed of discolored, old wood—some cherry with a dark stain and others a light shade of pine—and driftwood he found at the local creek. But Jack didn't care; it was a place for him to hang snakeskins and, of course, put Harley back into his aquarium.

Minutes passed as Jack played repeated games of darts with his collection of Swiss Army knives, before a familiar smell made its way up to his nose.

"Pizza!" Jack yelled.

For a moment, anyway, the horror of summer school melted away. The smell of tomatoes, pepperoni, garlic, and oregano was calling his name. Jack knew right where it was coming from, the kitchen window. His mom always cooled it off before serving.

Mom's so easy to read, Jack thought.

Jack slid down the rope, landing gracefully with two feet. He looked at the pizza sitting on the windowsill and the empty kitchen behind it. And there it was… steaming hot and already perfectly sliced into delicious triangles.

He approached the window and was just inches away. "This is too easy," he said, picking up a hot slice.

"Jack!" his mom yelled, popping up from what looked like the sink.

"Whoa!" Jack jolted back and dropped the slice on the ground.

"Jack, get in here right now!" Jack's mom yelled, pointing toward the kitchen table.

Jack put his head down and walked inside to the table. When he looked up, not only did he see his mom, but his dad was also glaring at him. Their arms were folded across their chests. This was the you're-in-some-bigtime-trouble pose.

"So do you have anything to say, Jack?" his dad asked. He was talking in his special dad voice, the one he only broke out on special occasions. Jack noticed that he was unbuttoning the cuffs of his dress shirt.

"Thanks for the pizza?" Jack said. He knew this was not the right answer.

"We mean about summer school," his mom said, shaking her head.

"Ah, yeah, you heard?" Jack tilted his head. He already knew the answer, of course, but he would use any stall tactic at this point.

"Of course, we did," Mom said. "Jack, you knew you were falling behind. We discussed it. You said you were going to do better."

Jack felt that like a stab in the chest. He did promise to do better. "Sorry, Mom." He picked a piece of pepperoni off his slice and popped it in his mouth.

"Sorry isn't enough this time," Dad said. "There have to be consequences."

Jack swallowed. "Umm, yeah, summer school, and it's not going to be fun. And you know, since it's really one big punishment itself, there's really no need for me to be grounded, right?"

"Your mother and I haven't yet determined that," his dad said. "But we really think you need to get your act together. This can't keep going on, Jack."

"I'll do better."

Jack's mom shook her head. It was a promise they had heard many times before. "Just... Just take your pizza and go to your room. Your father and I will discuss this and—"

"Sure thing," Jack said. "I'm going to my room. Right now." He scooped up his pizza and dashed to the stairway, almost stepping on Morgan again. "Sorry."

He flopped onto his bed and pulled his phone from his pocket. He texted Gene: *So far so good.*

Gene replied texted back: *U grounded?*

Jack wasn't quite sure how to answer that question. He bit into the pizza. It was so delicious. If he could get his mom's pizza every day, it would make summer school a little easier.

Jury still out, Jack texted.

Jack finished his pizza. He could hear his parents talking but couldn't make out their words. He hoped that their long deliberation meant they couldn't agree, and he might get off without being grounded. The anticipation was killing him, though. He walked toward the door and listened. Nothing. He crept closer to the stairwell. Nothing. He took three steps down and—

"Jack! Come down here," his father's voice boomed.

Jack swallowed. He took a deep breath and headed into the kitchen.

"Your mother and I have decided you'll have to do the dishes for the rest of the week, and no going out," his dad said. "I'll give you a week of freedom before summer school, but after it starts, you'll have to be in your room by seven o'clock every night. And you can forget Woodward."

"Wait. What?" Jack said, barely able to mingle the two words into a single complaint. "No Woodward? That's way too much, that's…"

His dad's eyebrows raised. It was a spooky eyebrow, that was for sure. His dad was usually pretty calm and collected. But when he got angry, that eyebrow seemed to act independently from the rest of his body.

"Never mind," Jack said. "What I meant to say was that's a fair punishment." He turned his attention to the pizza. Pizza had never yelled at him. Pizza had always been there for him, like a best friend.

"So, I was wondering," he said, almost afraid to ask. "My summer is wrecked. And I know, I know… it's all my fault. But since school isn't over for the summer yet, do you think I could go hang out with Gene after dinner?"

"No!" his dad said. "You can go to your room, though! Next week you can hang out with Gene."

"I understand." Jack put his head down. "I'm going to study anyways, and maybe take a nap in my room."

45

Jack gulped down the rest of the piece of pizza and went straight to his room. He shut and locked his door, immediately opened his window and dropped his bike into the backyard. Next, he opened his closet, dragged the mannequin over to his bed, and carefully tucked it under the blankets. Jack sat on his open windowsill and admired his bed. He chuckled before he leaped out the window and rode away.

As he rode down the street, the warm summer evening air hit his face. He could almost taste summer on his tongue. An interesting mix of lilac, honeysuckle, and pear trees filled the air. He took a deep breath in and exhaled. Freedom. Soon-to-be-summer freedom. But on this day, it was bittersweet. And maybe a tad more bitter than sweet.

Chapter 6
The Greatest Discovery of All Time

Jack arrived on his bike at their favorite place for stunts and track riding. It was a dusty field near the entrance to Boonetown Woods. He carefully raked the dirt on the track when Gene rolled his bike onto the scene. Jack switched from rake to shovel, using it to pack the jumps tight. They had made the little track themselves and took good care of it. Jack particularly enjoyed making the most dangerous jumps.

"Look at this," Gene said, slipping the bike pump out of the backpack on his shoulders.

"Awesome. You remembered this time."

The pump was a big deal to Jack because his back tire tended to go flat pretty often. He figured he'd need to buy a new one soon. If he mowed a few lawns over the summer, it shouldn't be a problem. Of course, his parents were going to have to let him out of his room to do that.

With the last jump mounded up and packed tight, Jack and Gene raced around the track with expert speed. They hit the jumps at speeds and angles that would surely have their mothers panicking. The bikes bounced and shuddered, chains whistled, and tires screamed. Jack only had to stop twice to use Gene's pump for his back tire.

Pedal, jump, lean right, berm, jump left, tuck, pedal, jump, pedal, and repeat. Like seasoned pilots in a cockpit, it was smooth flying until... *Turbulence.*

Jack heard a clanging noise and then Gene's voice screaming for about three seconds before a thump sound.

Jack turned just in time to see Gene flying over the handlebars. The first thump had been his bike hitting the ground. The second was Gene hitting the ground.

Jack jumped off his bike and ran to check on Gene. He passed by Gene's bike first and assessed the damage: a broken rim, a bent fork, and a loose chain. From the looks of it, he'd gotten out lucky. The only damage Jack could see was a scraped and bleeding elbow.

"Your elbow's bleeding, Gene."

"Yeah, yeah, I know. But I didn't even feel it." Gene got to his feet, brushing the dirt off his clothes, and inspecting his dusty glasses. The glasses had taken a beating before and seemed to have survived yet another mishap.

"Looks like your bike wasn't so lucky." Jack pointed to the wrangled mess.

"What did I hit?" Gene asked.

"I don't know, but whatever it was, it made for an awesome wreck."

They walked into the dust and scoped out the culprit. The dust from the accident had settled. They scouted out the area around the wrecked bike and the Gene-shaped smudge on the track. Then, directly beside the last jump

Jack had been packing down, they saw something sticking slightly up out of the dirt.

"It looks like a box," Gene said, looking at Jack.

Jack knocked on the object, an excited sort of smile crept over his face. "It's wooden. I think it might be hollow."

"You'd know that sound," Gene joked. "It would be just like your head."

Jack rolled his eyes. It would take a lot more than some lame joke to bring him down.

They dug around the edge of the box. It took a bit of work, as the box was much larger than Jack had thought upon first glance.

"This thing is pretty big, huh?" Gene asked.

"Yeah."

Jack thought it might be as big as a shoebox. But a bit more digging unearthed even more of it. They had managed to free two corners and a whole side. The box was more like a chest. It was made of mostly wood, with metal handles, and looked ancient.

"Maybe it's pirate's treasure," Jack said.

"Nah." Gene tapped the chest. "No pirates in Boonetown."

"Well, it's pretty old," Jack said. "Okay, let's yank it out."

Jack and Gene grabbed both ends.

"On the count of three..." Gene said.

Jack nodded. "One and two and three... Go."

Gene's and Jack's faces tensed as they pulled together. Pulling up against the tight grip of the old, packed dirt, their legs, arms, and veins bulged. The chest moved, but not much.

"Okay, okay… One more big tug," Jack said. "Can you, do it?"

Gene comically flexed his muscles and nodded. "Of course."

Jack grabbed the edge of the chest again. This time he took the time to look at it. It was weathered and a lighter wood shade with some markings that were covered by dirt. It also had a pair of metal handles on each side. He thought of what could be in it—some sort of treasure or old items his dad and grandpa might go nuts over—and it seemed to give him a little extra boost of strength.

Together, he and Gene tugged at the chest one more time. It wiggled, came free a bit, and then finally came loose. When it did, it almost looked like the ground had spat it out. Jack and Gene stumbled backward. Jack fell on his butt. The chest was free.

Gene and Jack jumped to their feet and hovered over the strange find.

"What do you think's in it?" Jack asked.

Gene shrugged his shoulders.

The possibilities were endless. Jack's brain already conjured up about a trillion things that could be inside.

They reached down together, both trying to open it at the same time. They smiled nervously and touched the lid.

Chapter 7
Treasure

Jack put his hand on the right side of the lid, and Gene took the left. They looked at one another with stirring excitement. Jack took a deep breath. Gene took a deep breath. They slowly started to open the lid and—

Boom... Crackle! Boom!

Both boys jumped. Jack even let out a rather embarrassing little scream.

"Thunder?" Gene asked. "But there's no rain in the forecast…"

More thunder rolled across the sky. This time bolts of lightning blossomed from the clouds that had turned violently gray.

"Great," Jack said. "Lightning."

Big, fat drops of rain started to fall, plopping them on the face. The raindrops picked up speed, hitting the ground in an almost musical way. Instantly the smell of cool rain hitting the hot earth filled their noses, the sweet smell of a summer storm.

"Let's get this thing to the bungalow," Gene said.

"Yeah," Jack agreed. "Help me get it."

"But it's lightning. And it has metal handles."

"Well, then, let's do it fast."

The boys grabbed on to the chest. It was a little harder to hold now that it was wet from the rain.

Under heavy sheets of rain and drumming thunder in the sky, Jack and Gene rushed as fast as they could, carrying the chest toward their secret bungalow.

The bungalow was deep into the woods. They would have to jump across a creek to reach it, which was one of the reasons Jack and Gene had been able to keep it a secret for so long. Spangler Creek really wasn't much of a creek at all—just wide enough to barely be able to cross with a solid jump, a jump both Jack and Gene were fully capable of.

Only now, with the pounding rain and carrying the heavy chest between them, the usually easy hike was proving to be a lot of work. The trees blocked some of the rain, but not much. The foliage on the ground had become slick, and much of the dirt was turning into mud. They nearly slipped a dozen times as they made their way down to the thin banks of Spangler Creek.

They dropped the chest on the way but managed to wrestle it off the ground and took off running for their creek and the bungalow beyond.

"Come on, Gene. We're almost there," Jack said, with streaks of mud under his eyes, looking like Native American war paint, and his clothes and sneakers now soaked with rain.

"I know," Gene shouted back. He was forced to tilt his head backward every now and then to make sure his glasses didn't go sliding off of his wet nose. Every time he did, his nose and mouth were filled with rainwater, nearly choking him. "I wish they made windshield wipers for glasses. That's what I'm going to do. I'll be rich."

One near-fall later, they were standing on the banks of Spangler's Creek. Jack had never seen the creek like this before. Usually, it was about knee-deep and about five feet across. But now, because of rainfall earlier in the week and this sudden downpour, it was like a totally different creek.

The water was now spilling over the banks. The water churned like it never had before.

"Holy crap!" Gene said. "It's rushing so fast. How can we cross it with this chest? You want to just open it here?"

Jack lived for moments like this. "No. There's gotta be a way."

"Are you sure? I've never seen the creek like this."

"Me neither." Jack looked around the banks, looking for anything that might help him across.

And there, about ten feet away from him, was a small tree, a thin, little oak that had yet to spread its branches out. Jack ran over and shimmied up it. The tree was barely big enough for him to climb; he could easily wrap his arms around it. As Jack climbed toward the top, it did exactly what he had hoped: it started to bend.

"Jack, get off of it!" Gene yelled.

Jack could barely hear him over the pouring rain. "I'll be fine."

"No way. It looks like that thing is going to break."

54

"I know," Jack yelled back. "That's the plan…"

The tree snapped, and Jack went sprawling to the ground, letting out a scream on the way. He landed on the opposite side of the creek, half in and half out of the water. The fall knocked the wind out of him. He got to his feet, panting and gasping for air.

"Jack. You okay?" Gene yelled.

"Uh-huh," Jack said. "All toes, fingers, arms, and legs accounted for. Just… whooo… need to catch my breath."

"You made a bridge."

Wincing, Jack said, "I know. Trust me, I know my stuff."

"Although, really," Gene said, "it's more like a tightrope."

"Whatever. Come on… Let's get this thing across. I'm getting soaked."

That was an understatement. His shoes were absolutely drenched. They squished with every step. Jack crossed back over to the other side of the creek, which was looking more and more like a river. As he crossed, he realized that perhaps the tree was not wide enough; he could barely place an entire foot on it without slipping off the side. Getting the chest across would be a huge chore.

"Go slow," Jack said.

They stepped onto the makeshift bridge. It started out fine, but when they were halfway across, the rain pounded even harder. It pelted them on their heads and slapped at the creek as if someone was tossing rocks into the water. Jack checked the banks on both sides and realized that it was not going to take long before the water came up over the outstretched tree—washing it and them both away.

"We have to hurry now," he said.

Gene nodded, and they both put some extra speed into their steps. Each step made Jack afraid that he'd slip and fall into the creek at any moment, but he somehow managed to make it to the other side. When he did, the water had just started to touch the bottom of the outstretched tree.

Gene took a big step forward. And it was then that a large pop noise filled their ears, almost as loud as the pounding rain. Jack saw that the tree-bridge had split right at the end. The only thing holding it together was a little, banana peel-thin piece of bark. There was no way it would support Gene.

Trying his best to help, Jack grabbed the chest tightly. "Let go. Save yourself."

Gene released his end of the chest, and Jack pulled it forward. He pulled a little too hard and he stumbled back, slipping in the mud, and once again falling on his butt.

"Wow, I don't know my own strength," Jack said.

The sudden change in weight threw Gene off. He was fighting for balance, pinwheeling his arms, but it did no good. All Jack could do was watch his friend tumble into the water.

When he splashed down, he flailed his arms. Jack was pretty sure the water wasn't very deep—not yet anyway—and was certain Gene could touch the bottom. He reached for Gene's hand over the water. Gene grabbed it easily enough, and Jack pulled. It was a messy and wet ordeal, but Jack was able to get Gene out of the water. They scrambled to safety with their treasure at their feet.

"Thanks, man," Gene said, panting for breath.

"Sure. Are you good?"

"Yeah. But, oh, man… my glasses."

Jack punched Gene's shoulder. "What is that, like the tenth pair you've lost?"

"Oh, shut up. Now come on. Let's get out of this miserable rain."

Jack gave a quick thumbs-up before grabbing the chest. He dragged it forward as Gene got behind it and pushed. Together, they moved the chest along the wet and muddy ground. It was much easier than trying to carry it. They pushed the chest up the crest of one last hill while the lightning crackled above. Soon the glorious and familiar sight of their bungalow was in front of them. "Home away from home," Jack said.

Gene let out a sigh of relief. "Thank God!"

The bungalow wasn't much, but Jack was proud of it. As far as he was concerned, it was Boonetown's version of the Taj Mahal. It was also the labor of Jack's and Gene's evening hours and weekends. The bungalow consisted of a ten-by-twenty-foot tarp, hung and ratchet strapped between two trees. But the décor is what really made it feel like home for them.

An old, weathered wooden telephone line spool made a great table. The chairs were nothing more than tree stumps, cut up from a fallen white maple. The insides of the tarp were covered with Southwestern blankets to give a cozy sort of feel, an earthy vibe, Jack had said.

"Whoa…" Jack exhaled, after wiping off the chest. "Look, Gene, there's a flag painted on the side."

They checked out the flag emblem, a simple blue background with a red cross standing right in the center.

"Yeah," Gene said. "I think I remember seeing that red cross before in Mr. Smith's history class. I remember the white diagonals with the blue in the background. I'm pretty sure this is the British flag. But I remember there being red lines inside of the white diagonals extending to the corners, though. Maybe they rubbed off?"

"Oh, yeah, Gene. Uh-huh, I'm pretty sure it is," Jack joked, knowing full well he most likely slept through that lesson.

Still, Jack was pretty sure Gene was right since Gene was the champion of anything school related. It was indeed the British flag, but they could tell it was different. It looked very old.

"Are we going to open it or what?" Jack asked.

"Sure thing."

With a little force, the lid popped open.

There was almost a sound to their disappointment, sort of like the sound a balloon makes when it pops. Jack stared into the trunk, irritated. "All that work… for this?"

Chapter 8
The Letter

"I know I lost my glasses," Gene said. "But I'm seeing that right… Right? Is that just… just… It's just a stupid envelope?"

"Awww, seriously," Jack said. "I thought it was heavy because of all the treasure inside."

"Me too." Gene gave the chest a little kick. "And it's just a dumb letter."

Jack snagged the envelope out of the chest. It was sealed, but there was something inside of it, something light and square in shape. The envelope looked very old. Instead of crisp white, like most envelopes, this one was almost yellow and very dirty. There was no name or address.

Jack tore open the envelope and carefully pulled out a folded sheet of paper that was also thin and yellowed. Sure, it was a far cry from gold and treasure, but it was still pretty sweet to have found something this old and to be the first to see it.

He unfolded the paper and then let out a sigh.

"What is it?" Gene asked.

"It's in cursive. Neat and pretty cursive."

Gene snickered, doing his best not to break into full-out laughter. "That's right. Poor Jack can't read cursive."

"Shut up, Gene. I don't have time to learn that kind of stuff. I can't be great at everything. Anyway… You think you can read it, even without your glasses?"

"Let me see." He took the letter from Jack and held it very close to his face, so close that his nose almost touched it. "Holy crap! This letter is dated 28 June 1745. That's before our country was even the United States."

"Well, read it." Jack gave Gene a nudge to the shoulder.

Gene cleared his throat and read the letter in an English accent:

Dear Whomever,

This is Thomas Hubbs, redcoat, and member of the Virginia Colony. I am writing this today to inform you that I have been met with an unfortunate incarceration at the hands of the Shawnee Indians. However, I was fortunate to have made acquaintances with two Shawnee men, who told me many fascinating things about their great culture. Unfortunately, Chief Nozuka was not pleased about what they've told me. So, I and the two Shawnee men have been incarcerated and will be sacrificed tonight at the strike of dusk. I wish to tell my wife Elizabeth, my son Jonathan, and daughter Maryliza that I love them and miss them so. Jonathan, I hope you become a strong, noble man, and that you will please take care of the family. My family lives in Southwest London, near Pennington Square. Please pass this on to them —

"Too late," Jack laughed.

"Dude, have some respect for once." Gene shook his head, then cleared his throat and continued to read:

Also, it is my duty to pass on the secret information that has been passed on to me and, unfortunately, has put me in this predicament. The Shawnee believe that they must always give back to their god. One of the ways that their tribe has given back is by burying a treasure full of the finest jewels and gold in the land. By doing so, they believe that their god will reward them with fertile soil and clothe them with eternal life. Therefore, enclosed in this envelope is a map, which leads to the treasure. But one must be careful; one must pass over a fatal river full of massive turbulent rapids to find the treasure. This is a task that should not be taken lightly. I hope all is well with you, and if you find the treasure, please share with my family, whom I love dearly.

Yours truly,
Thomas Hubbs

P.S. Excuse the heavy chest. It was the only thing I could find to preserve these notes.

"Yeah, he better be sorry about the chest," Jack said. "I almost tore a bicep lugging that thing through the woods."

Gene shot him a look that was classic Gene. It was Gene's *would-you-shut-up* face. He used it only when he was really annoyed, and right now it was drilling a hole through him.

"Enough joking, Jack. Do you know how big a discovery this is? This could make national news."

"But it's not going to," Jack said.

"What? Seriously, what are you saying?"

"Gene... there's a map, right here." He shook the envelope a bit and caught the map as it fell out. It was folded tightly into a square. The paper was faded and just as old-looking as the letter. "A map that will lead us to treasure."

"I don't know, Jack. We may want to go to the authorities with this one," Gene said, crossing his arms.

"No, you may want to listen to *my* authority when I say *we* are finding this treasure. If we get police or other adults involved, the treasure will be found and end up in some stuffy, old museum."

"And what will we do with it if we find it?" Gene asked.

"I don't know. Let's find out." He gave his friend a winning smile, one that had won Gene over more times than he could count. He could see Gene's expression softening and knew that it had worked again.

"Fine," Gene said. "Open the map."

Jack gently unfolded the thin, porous papyrus-like paper from its sixteen folded subsections. Plopping it on the ground, the two of them stared intently at it, noticing some geographical landmarks right away.

"Oh, wow," Jack said, tapping near the left side of the map. "I know right where this starts. That's Pilot Rock... Right by Shoemaker's Farm, where they sell the peaches."

"Hey, you're right," Gene said. "There should be a trail or at least an opening that leads right into the Gauley. It's maybe three miles away, tops. But the hard part will be crossing the Great Gauley River. My mom says someone drowns in that thing every year."

"Yeah, but we'll be careful," Jack said.

"Dude, we could barely cross that little creek to get *here.*"

Jack gave Gene a good-natured thump on the arm as they looked the map over. "Look... We can do this. We know the landmarks, we know the town, and at the risk of sounding all kinds of cheesy, we make a good team."

Jack knew that Gene was not a complete worrywart. He was just the more logical of the two. Whereas Jack was fine to jump into something without thinking, Gene usually tried to take a moment to think things over. But in this case, it seemed the idea of hidden treasure was too much to resist.

"You're right," Gene finally said. "We could do it. But that Gauley scares me. Dude, the Gauley has class-five rapids. Some of the best kayakers in the world can't

64

even handle it. You can get stuck in the undertow and never come up."

"Cool," Jack said. "Sounds like fun. I knew you would be up for it."

Gene gave a desperate little sigh and shrugged. "So, when do we start? And what should we pack?"

"Hmm... Sleeping bags, food, enough clothes for maybe two days."

"Only two days?" Gene asked. "You think that's all it'll take?"

"Okay, maybe three. But we have to go as soon as school lets out for the summer," Jack said. "My dad gave me a week of freedom before summer school."

Gene squinted toward the now setting sun.

"So, how can we go on a camping trip without our parents knowing?" Gene asked.

"Gene, why are you asking all these questions?" Jack shot back.

Gene looked at Jack, with his hands in the air, laughing. "These are pretty good questions if you ask me. I mean, that may come up, you think?"

Jack needed a moment to think. A few minutes passed with not a word spoken. There was only the sound of water droplets from the tree limbs, pitter-pattering against their tarp roof until...

"Squeaker?" Gene asked.

"No way!" Jack said, rolling his eyes. "I'm not wiping his butt the whole trip! That's not the kind of treasure I'm after."

"Yeah, agreed," Gene said with a smile, "Nor do I want to smell it."

"Tim?" Gene asked.

"No, he bailed on me during the Bombgardner thing," Jack said.

Another minute of silence passed.

"I got it," Gene said, his face lit up. "I'll call Edgar. He has an older brother who can vouch as his dad. Our parents will never know."

The mere mention of Edgar made Jack grimace. Edgar Crumm was a friend of Gene's, but Jack had never cared for the kid. He was quiet and weird. He was also one of those kids who did not believe in personal space, chewed with his mouth open, and always smelled like a dirty shoe.

Jack stared at Gene and shook his head. "No way. I don't want anything to do with that kid. He's weird and all he does is stutter. And his face is rounder than a bowling ball. I always feel like it's going to roll off his head."

"Jack, that's rude. And he's not that weird," Gene said, before quickly changing his tune. "Okay, okay. It's not like I ever really talk to him, but his mom's always gone, and he lives with his brother. His brother can help us. Really, he's cool. He won't rat us out."

Jack sat on one of the stump chairs. He grabbed the emergency bag of cookies they always kept on a small shelf they'd built from old wood. "But if we get his brother, Edgar will want to come," Jack said. He offered Gene a cookie.

"Probably." Gene took the cookie. "But if we can get the help from his brother, I say it's worth it."

Jack thought about it for a moment. He downed three cookies. He knew that Gene liked Edgar quite a bit and that he probably didn't like using the kid as leverage. But here they were, with the chance to find treasure. This was a big deal that called for a big plan. A big secret plan.

"Fine," Jack said. "If toting Edgar around on our treasure hunt is the price we have to pay, fine. But don't expect me to talk to him or anything. That kid bugs me."

Jack looked at the treasure map. Excitement was building inside him. Who cared if dumb old Edgar might be tagging along? They had a real-life treasure map… to a treasure that wasn't all that far away.

Even with summer school looming over him like some killer giant or Mrs. Bombgardner, Jack's prospects for a great summer just got a lot brighter.

Chapter 9
Best Laid Plans

Jack and Gene waited for the creek to subside before even attempting to go home. And besides, they needed a plan, a way to get to the treasure without getting sucked under those class-five rapids in the Gauley. They spent the time knocking ideas back and forth until they finally came up with the perfect plan: Jack would supply all of the gear needed to find the treasure successfully, and Gene would get the parents on board with the trip.

"So, we agree?" Jack asked.

Gene nodded. "Agreed."

They even shook hands on the deal, making the whole scheme solid, solid as the rocks they'd have to climb.

They planned to leave on Friday, June 12th, the day after school let out for the summer. Jack had a few days of freedom, and as he told Gene, "I can't think of a better way to spend it than treasure hunting." They planned to return home on June 15th, which gave them three days to find their treasure, which, according to Jack, was "More than enough time."

It was Jack's idea to tell Edgar's brother that they were going to the Chesapeake to do some crabbing. To get all the stars aligned, Gene would call Edgar later that night, and then Edgar's brother would call Gene's parents. Jack was more than convinced his parents would let him go if Gene's parents endorsed the trip. They were always complaining that he didn't get enough of the great outdoors. This was perfect.

Jack folded the map and tucked it into his pocket as carefully as he could. The smell of summer and freshly fallen rain was in the air, amplified by the promise of a big adventure. They hopped the creek, hurried back to get their bikes, and headed home. Jack pedaled. Gene had to carry his broken bike the whole way.

***

Gene carried what was left of his bike into the garage. His mom was standing there waiting for him.

"Gene. What happened? You're soaking wet and covered in mud. And your bike. Is that your bike?"

"Jack and I got stranded in the rain. I sort of… Well, I sort of got soaked."

"And covered in mud?"

"Yeah, that too. I wrecked my bike and spilled out into a mud puddle, and my glasses broke. But before I had time to pick them up, the rain washed them away."

Gene's mom rolled her eyes. "The rain washed them away?"

Gene really didn't like to lie, but he felt he had to tell a little lie to work his way up to the big one later that night.

"That's terrible, sweetie," his mom said. "Well, don't worry about it. I'll get you an eye appointment tomorrow. I'm just glad you're all right."

"Thanks, Mom."

"Okay, get inside and get cleaned up. Put a Band-Aid on your elbow." They walked inside together, chatting a bit, before Gene ran upstairs to take a shower.

Chapter 10
The Accomplice

Edgar was watching TV and eating a frozen pizza when the phone rang. His older brother was still at work, which meant Edgar had the entire place to himself. It was a small house and a pretty messy one, filled with empty cans, bags of sugar, and dried up mixing bowls with whisks covered in cake batter, but Edgar didn't care. He knew he had a pretty sweet deal, living with his older brother. Some of the kids at school thought it was weird, and a lot of his friends could not come over to hang out because their parents did not trust the living situation. But he was cool with that.

Edgar checked the time. It was before seven o'clock, which meant the call wasn't for his brother. So, did that mean it was for him? *Weird.* Edgar didn't get many calls.

"Hello?" he said.

"Yo, Edgar. It's Gene. What are you up to?"

"N-Not a whole l-lot. J-Just watching some TV. W-What about you?"

"Funny you should ask," Gene said. "You got big plans this summer?"

"No. N-N-None at all." Edgar slowed down. He had a persistent stutter.

"Well, if you want, I think I've got a little adventure for you."

Edgar felt his heart speed up a little. An adventure? No one ever asked Edgar to do much of anything, let alone an adventure. "W-What is it?" He thought he'd better be cautious.

"Well, Jack and I were riding our bikes, and we found a chest with a map that leads to a treasure."

"N-No way," Edgar said. "A tr-treasure map? R-Really?"

"Yes, really. The map is pretty old, but Jack and I figured out where it leads. But here's the thing: it's going to take two, maybe three days to get there and make it back home. We'll need your brother to vouch for us so we can find it. You think he would do that for us?"

"V-Vouch for what?"

Gene let go a sigh. "Look, I'll explain it in detail later, but we just need your brother to pretend he's your dad. Then he'll tell our parents that we'll be with him… and you."

"O-Okay," Edgar said. "I guess s-s-so, but why the lie?"

Gene shared the details of their plan and how they thought it might all work out. Edgar listened, very excited now, hanging on every little detail.

"S-So w-why do we n-need my br-brother, again?" Edgar asked when Gene was finished.

"We're going to need him to pretend he is your dad when he calls our parents."

"Oh, sh-sh-sure. He'd do that. Now, h-hold on… You said we're cr-cr-crabbing?"

There was a small pause on the other end before Gene answered.

"Yeah, sure, that's what your brother is going to tell our parents. That way nobody but us knows about the treasure."

Edgar wasn't crazy about lying, but if it meant he'd get to go on an adventure, then sure. He'd go along.

"W-When does my brother n-n-need to call?" Edgar asked.

"Within the next hour or two."

"O-Okay. He's s-still at work now, but sh-should be h-home soon."

"Great," Gene said.

Gene sounded very excited and that, in turn, made Edgar very excited. Gene gave him Jack's number so his brother could call his parents. When he hung up the phone, Edgar felt a wide smile stretch across his face. One that was so wide, it nearly hurt.

For the first time in a long time, Edgar felt alive, like he was truly part of something big. Edgar sat back down on the couch and unmuted the TV.

He watched a few cartoons before Julio got home.

"What's up, dork?" Julio asked.

"A lot, actually. L-L-Look… Can you d-d-do me a f-favor?"

Julio plopped down on the couch, purposely crowding Edgar.

"I don't know, man. What kind of a favor?"

Edgar told Julio the wild plan that Gene and Jack had come up with. He left the part about the potential treasure out because he didn't want Julio trying to tag along or making fun of them. But he had no trouble convincing Julio to go along with the scheme. Julio enjoyed a good caper from time to time.

Chapter 11
Boonetown Bandits

The morning light bent through the blinds of Jack's room. Jack's body was sprawled out, tangled in the covers while he hid from the lure of sunlight. He was far too preoccupied with the pleasant dream he was having of Sarah. Jack smiled thinly as his dream-self leaned in for a kiss. Closer... closer...

BEEP. BEEP. BEEP. BEEP...

His alarm clock was much more demanding than sunlight through his blinds. Jack sprung up. He glared at the alarm clock and slapped it to the floor. Jack wiped the eye boogers from his eyes and stumbled out of bed.

Any last bits of sleepiness disappeared when he realized what day it was: June 12th. School was over for the summer, well, for most kids, but right now that didn't matter. Jack had something much more important going on. He had started packing his backpack last night but decided sleep was more important. He finished packing his pack, shoving in underwear, socks, and body spray... *just in case* he happened to run into Sarah.

Jack grabbed his pack and headed downstairs to the kitchen, hoping that his parents had not changed their minds. He knew he was in trouble for the remainder of the summer and also knew he was fortunate his parents allowed him to go on the trip.

He crammed snacks into his bag while his parents sipped their morning coffee.

"Bye, Mom." He kissed her cheek and then gave his dad a hug.

"Have fun," his dad said. "And make sure to bring us back some crabs."

Jack swallowed as he remembered the lie he'd told them.

"Sure, Dad."

"And don't forget… This is it. No more trips this summer. When you get back home, you are officially grounded."

"Yeah, yeah." Jack looked at his sneakers. "I know."

Jack waved one last goodbye and bolted out of the front door, already trying to figure out how in the world he was supposed to come across a bushel of crabs.

A huge grin spread across his face when he saw Gene coming out of his house at the exact same time.

***

Arriving at Shoemaker's Farm, they stopped when they heard loud music blasting over the hill. It started as a murmur but then became louder, punctuated by the pumping and thumping of bass accompanied with the sound of vibrating bumpers. An old maroon Cadillac came into view, kicking plumes of dust into the air.

"What the heck is that thing?" Jack asked, coughing from the dust.

"That's a car, genius," Gene said.

"Yeah, but who's driving it?"

"I think that's Edgar's brother."

Sure enough, the car came to a screeching stop, and Edgar stepped out. The driver gave a little toot of his horn before speeding away. All three boys shielded themselves with their arms from the flecks of gravel that shot up into the air.

"Hey, Edgar. My pal," Jack said, even though he didn't really mean it.

"H-Hey," Edgar said. It was clear that Edgar had no idea how to take Jack.

Jack and Gene had been friends forever. But Edgar—well, Edgar was always on the outside looking in. Gene did his best sometimes to include Edgar in things, but Jack always felt awkward around Edgar. He never knew quite how to act or what to say.

The three guys just kind of stood there for a minute, looking at each other until Jack, who never liked awkward silences, said, "Well, then... Looks like we're off on the trip. So, let's go be bold. Just do what you're told. Let's go find some gold. So, give me a G, give me an O, give me an L, and a D. What's that spell?"

Edgar and Gene looked on, horrified at Jack's song and dance routine.

"Wow..." was all Gene could say.

Jack rolled his eyes and started walking.

"Whatever. Let's get going."

"Should we check the map first?" Gene asked.

"Yeah, yeah," Jack said. "Hold up. It's in my pack." Jack shrugged his backpack off and unzipped the front pocket. He pulled the old, fragile document from its hiding spot.

"Whoa!" Edgar said. "It l-l-looks... ancient. Wh-Wh-Where'd you g-guys find it?"
Gene patted Edgar on the back. "Let's just say I kind of ran into it."

Jack laughed. "He sure did. He fell head over heels for it."

Edgar just shook his head. "Okay. D-Don't t-t-tell me."

"I'll fill you in later," Gene said.

Jack unfolded the map. He pointed to the big X. "That's our destination. We should head south."

Gene agreed, and so did Edgar, and off they went at a pretty good clip.

"So, guys," Jack said, "we should come up with a name for us. Like a team name or something."

"For real?" Gene said.

Jack wasn't sure why Gene was being so sour. Maybe he thought he was trying a little too hard to not show his true feelings toward Edgar. But Jack had already decided to give the kid a chance. No sense in letting him ruin this awesome adventure.

"No, I'm serious. Everyone who has ever set forth on a journey has given themselves a name," Jack said.

"Think about it. The Three Musketeers... The Nature Boys, Road Warriors, um..."

"Hmm..." Gene said. "The Nature Boys, and the Road Warriors? What is that even? Old wrestlers. Like from my dad's time. The olden days."

"The Th-Three M-Musket-teers" Edgar said. "I'm p-pretty sure that's l-like an adventure s-s-story."

"Yeah, Dumas wrote it. I read it," Gene said.

"Okay, there, Dumas," Jack interrupted. "It's a movie, not a book, and it's better known as a candy bar. Or that's all anyone cool knows them as. Anyway, you nerds pay *way* too much attention in school. Maybe I'll just call you guys The Nerds," Jack laughed.

"And we'll call you Summer School," Gene said, nudging Jack's arm. "And it's pronounced Dew-ma."

Edgar couldn't keep from laughing. Then, as if trying to make up for the laughter, he blurted out, "H-How about the B-Boonetown Bandits?"

Jack looked too stunned to say anything. Gene, however, was quick to give credit where it was due. "Edgar, dude, that's a great name."

"Yeah," Jack said. "Great job, man. Yes. Jack Mathias and the Boonetown Bandits."

Gene looked at Edgar and then back to Jack. "Really? How about this, either the Boonetown Bandits, or... the Gryffindors" Gene smiled at Jack, knowing their opposing views on Harry Potter.

Jack's jaw dropped. "Oh, no! Nope! No way. I never liked those movies. Okay, the Boonetown Bandits it is!"

So onward the Boonetown Bandits marched in unison into the great outdoors. As they came closer to the edge of the farm field, they stopped to check the map. After some deliberation, they decided they should head southeast, down the descending end of the field.

Even though he didn't like to admit that sometimes he enjoyed how amazing and pretty nature was, Jack couldn't help himself.

"Wow. It's so nice here. The colors are so… so—"

Gene punched his shoulder. "What? Pretty. Does Jack like the pretty flowers?"

Jack rubbed his shoulder, even though it didn't hurt. "No, I was going to say vibrant."

"Th-They sure are," Edgar said. "And I c-can sm-smell pine and honeysuckle and l-lilacs."

Jack chuckled. "What are you? A bloodhound?"

They laughed before each took a deep breath of the fresh air.

The Boonetown Bandits were blazing their own path into the great unknown.

Chapter 12
The Adventure Begins

The grassy field eventually led to a scraggly woodland area with a path or two, which the boys knew pretty well. But they had never ventured as far into the woods as they were about to today.

Jack stopped at the edge of the woods. "Okay, we need to find the falls first. It's a bit of a hike, so let's take our time."

The Boonetown Bandits set out on the hiking path. When they rounded the next bend, they heard the river in the distance. With each step, the sound grew from a faint background noise until gradually, over the next quarter mile, it turned into a full roar. As they drew even closer, the air grew damp and soon the mist could be seen in the air and felt on their faces.

It was a nice break from the heat. While the day wasn't really all that hot, walking directly under the sun had started to take its toll on them.

"That feels nice," Jack said. He raised his head to the sky and let the mist from the falls land on his face.

"It sure does." Gene wiped the sweat off his forehead and wiped his glasses on his shirt.

Edgar leaned back, too. "It's l-l-like a sh-shower."

They walked for a few more minutes until Pilot Rock came into view. As they approached the landmark, Jack couldn't contain his thoughts.

"Wow! I've only seen pictures of this place. It's amazing."

Gene stopped walking, too. "It's even better than the pictures."

"Check out the river," Jack said. "It's moving so fast..." The rush of water tore around Pilot Rock, creating a vicious set of rapids.

Gene pointed to the white caps. "Wow! Look at it, guys. Those rapids are crazy."

"And sc-scary," Edgar added.

"Come on," Jack said, with a wave of his hand. "Let's get up on the rock and see what it looks like from up there. The rock hangs out over the river. So cool."

"I don't know," Gene said. "Are you sure? I mean, is it safe?"

Jack took off toward the rock. "Of course, it's safe. The rock's been standing here for eons. Like a million years. You know that."

The three shuffled out to the very edge of Pilot Rock, which hung over the river. It looked almost like a small gorge.

"This is wild," Gene said. "We can almost touch the water."

"Don't reach too far," Jack said. "You'll get sucked in."

Gene laughed. "That's not true. Come on, Edgar, get closer to the edge."

Edgar shook his head. "N-Nope."

A red-tailed hawk screeched overhead and blasted down toward the water. Its talons cut through the surface, grasping and ripping out a lively brook trout. The hawk, with its auburn feathers and white underbelly, flew back overhead with the spotted trout flapping in its beak.

"Whoa! Savage! Like in the real sense of the word..." Gene said with wide eyes.

Meanwhile, Jack paced around and skipped small rocks into the water, anxious to get on with the adventure. "This is cool, but we got some gold to find."

The Bandits agreed, and they continued along the trail.

"Hold up," Gene said. "Let me take a picture." He wrestled his phone out of his bag while he ran. He stopped and set up the perfect camera angle. "I should have taken the picture when we were on the rock."

"Gene, I told you before, no phones allowed," Jack said. He knew how much of a bummer he sounded, but he didn't care. "When you go in the woods, you can't have a phone. Imagine if Columbus rolled up to America with a phone in his hand. He would have been like: 'Google Maps said I'm in San Salvador; turn around, men. Asia's the other way.'"

Gene shook his head. "Well, he named it San Salvador, so how would Google Maps have known beforehand? Also, how would Google have been a company if they originated in California, which hadn't technically been discovered yet?"

"Gene, the point is, no real explorers ever used phones. Like Columbus, Magellan, umm... Lewis and Fart wouldn't have either."

"Lewis and Clark, you mean?" Gene asked.

"Nerd! Don't interrupt! So really, anyone who went into the woods who wasn't lame wouldn't have used a phone, you dork. And besides, we're 'unplugging.' That way, our parents can't trace us, stupid!" Jack said, revealing the true reason he didn't want to bring phones. "Give me that phone, dork."

"Never."

Jack's and Gene's voices blended together. They rolled around the rock, trying to pry the phone from each other's hands. Several rolls and bruises later, Jack got the upper hand.

"We have a winner," Jack said. "Weighing in at one hundred and twenty-five pounds: Jack Mathias."

Jack tossed the phone in the air and caught it behind his back. He tossed it again, but this time the phone bounced off his hand, then bounced off his foot, then off the rock, then *SPLASH* into the water.

"What the...? Jack, my new phone! You idiot. What were you thinking?" Gene hollered, while his face was fuming.

Jack looked on in horror. "Oh, wow! Jeez. That just happened. I'm sorry, man."

"Yeah, that just happened, Jack. And there's no way to make it un-happen either!" Gene yelled.

"It should have never ricocheted off my foot like that, Gene. That was like a one-in-a-thousand chance."

"When this trip is over, we aren't talking the rest of the summer. You ruin everything. I don't know why I'm even friends with you." Gene stepped away from Jack. "Come on, Edgar. Let's go."

Edgar shrugged and followed Gene.

Jack peered into the rushing water for a moment before running to catch up with them. He really did feel bad and promised to replace the phone, somehow.

The Boonetown Bandits walked quietly along the riverside trail. They didn't say too much. Jack tried to talk to Gene, but he was still too angry to respond. The lighthearted excitement that began the journey was replaced with tension, a tug-of-war rope between a group of sumo wrestlers.

"Come on," Jack said. "We have a long way to go. Please. Talk to me."

Nothing livened up the crew until…

"Wow, look at that!" Gene pointed in the air. The three looked up at the old rope bridge extending high above the water. Looming underneath the bridge, a series of cascading waterfalls and class-five rapids awaited. The water tumbled over massive boulders and churned white underneath.

"That's awesome. That bridge looks super sketchy," Jack said, yelling over the crashing water.

"It kinda reminds me of that movie with the pirates—oh, wait, who was that actor?" Gene asked.

"You're right," Jack said. "I can't remember his name either."

Gene smacked Jack's shoulder. "It's all right, man. I know it was an accident."

"Thanks," Jack said. "I'll replace the phone, somehow." He snapped his fingers. "When we get all that gold. I'll buy you a new phone. Heck, I'll buy you ten new phones."

"Yeah, yeah," Gene said. "Think. What is that actor's name? I hate it when I can't remember stuff. It'll bug me all day."

He broke off a small branch and tossed it into the water. "He always wears crazy wardrobes and looks like a pirate even when he's not playing one," Gene said.

The Bandits laughed but settled down when they heard an unusual noise in the distance.

"Wait." Gene tugged on Jack's arm. "I hear the rapids, but what's that high-pitched noise? Listen…"

The three scanned the rope bridge. An old, rotten two-by-four broke from the bridge, falling end over end through the air before splashing into the rapids below.

"Oh, wow!" Gene cried. "Look!"

"What is that?" Jack asked, squinting into the sun.

"You see the hooves hanging?" Gene asked. "It's a deer stuck on the bridge. If he falls, he's a goner."

"Let's save him." Jack scanned for the fastest way up the bank to the bridge. "This way, guys," he urged, pointing up the worn path. The three quickly scurried up the steep bank to the hiking path and stopped in front of the bridge.

"Whoa! The bridge is a lot higher up from this view, guys," Gene said, huffing and puffing.

"Y-Yeah," Edgar agreed. He bent at the waist and tried to catch his breath.

"Yeah, I'd say," Jack said. "Well, we have to go across it anyway for the gold, so I guess now's the time." The three knelt as Jack drew the plan in the dirt. "Here's the deal. Gene, you go in front of me. Edgar, you stay at the end here. If the bridge breaks somehow, make sure you anchor yourself to the land and hold on to the bridge so we can climb back to land."

Gene looked at Jack. "Why do I have to go first? Why can't you?"

"You're the lightest. Trust me, I'll be right behind you to catch you if something happens," Jack said, before turning to Edgar, "And no offense, Edgar, but you're our anchor. We need you. But if you take one step on this bridge, this whole thing will be driftwood in a matter of seconds. Nothing personal, man."

Edgar's cheeks turned red as he smiled. "N-Nothing personal."

Stepping out onto the swaying bridge, Gene's and Jack's knuckles turned white as they clenched the weathered rope handrails. They stepped in unison across the bridge.

"Man, I don't know. Jack, this rope doesn't look very strong. That sapling across Spangler's Creek might be an upgrade compared to this," Gene yelled over the sound of the whitewater below.

"Yeah, the rope looks a bit on the frayed side, Gene. But honestly, compared to the rotted wood boards we're standing on, the rope isn't that bad."

With the bridge swaying from side to side, Jack continued to try and lighten the mood. "You know, why didn't the forest service ever put some wood sealer on these things?"

Gene let go a small nervous chuckle.

Jack and Gene shimmied to the middle of the bridge, Gene leading the way, terrified. He held his breath; his mouth was dry and had a metallic taste. His legs quivered and his body shook with every step. The bridge shook even more. The deer did nothing to help the matter. It moved its head back and forth, letting out a higher pitched scream than before.

"Oh, jeez," Jack said. "That poor thing. We have to save him."

"Jack?" Gene said, his voice tender. "All we can do is try."

Jack looked ahead at the deer. "We're coming for you, just be calm. Have no fear, Jack Mathias is here." Jack smiled and took one more step before... *Snap.*

The wood below Jack's feet broke.

"Gene," Jack yelled, wide-eyed. He fell through the bridge.

Gene grabbed the side rope and lunged down, grabbing Jack's fingers. "Got ya!" Gene held on to Jack's hand, saving him from plummeting to his death.

"Holy crap!" Jack yelled in a panic. "I'm too young to die."

"Jack, it'll be all right, man. I got you, bud. We're going to get through this," Gene said.

"W-We g-got you," Edgar called.

Jack's feet dangled. He held on to Gene's hand. Slowly, the sweat between Jack's and Gene's hands loosened their grips, and their hands slipped apart. The startled deer kicked its legs out to the side and sliced the rope with its hooves.

"Jack, re-grip! You're slipping. Oh, no, Jack!" Gene yelled and looked on in horror. And then suddenly…

Snap. The side ropes broke, splitting the bridge in half.

"Aagh!" Jack and Gene screamed as they plummeted toward the water on the bridge-turned-rope-swing. Like a missile, they headed full speed into the side of the cliff and… *bang.* Jack's and Gene's bodies crashed into the rock ledge. Jarred loose from their grip, the two fell. Jack stretched out his hands. He grasped the second-to-last wood plank, just a few feet above the deer. Quickly Jack spotted Gene, and he shot out his hand to catch him. "Gene!"

As if in slow motion, their hands reunited, but the bridge's movement forced their fingers apart.

Gene fell. "No-No!" Jack and Edgar cried out. Gene looked up in horror, falling and plummeting until... *Splat.*

Gene let out a high-pitched, death-curdling scream, loud enough to make dogs in neighboring states bark. Jack and Edgar looked down in shock at the massacre while the deer screamed almost as loud as Gene.

Gene's body somehow never touched the water. Instead, Jack and the deer held on to the rotted boards, hanging over the massive waterfalls, and Gene's only hope for survival was his underwear that was now caught around the deer's velvety antlers.

"Holy crap, Gene! Now that's a super-wedgie if I ever saw one," Jack yelled.

"H-H-Hold on!" Edgar yelled. "The b-bridge screws are c-c-coming loose."

Edgar latched on to the end of the bridge with a bear hug as it ripped out of the ground. Jack, the deer, and Gene got a sudden one-foot bungee drop, which in Gene's case almost made his underwear part of his anatomy. But luckily Edgar's lumbering weight and strength were strong enough to hold on.

Jack looked up at Edgar. "You're the man, Edgar. You got this. Just hold on. I'm gonna climb up."

Jack planned his ascent to the top of the cliff. "All right, Gene, once I get up, we'll pull you guys up to safety." But when he reached for the next board... *Snap.*

The board broke, and Jack was not ascending anymore. He was descending.

"Aagh!" Jack yelled as he plummeted, flailing his arms and legs. Gene reached out his hand. Jack's hand stretched, and just in the nick of time, they locked hands.

"Whoa!" Jack yelled, scared and clinging on for life. "Holy crap!" Jack looked up at Gene. "That's some strong underwear you got on, man!"

Gene, in agony and pain, stared blankly into Jack's eyes.

"Gene, you okay?" Jack asked, assessing the situation. "I'd hate to say this, but the best chance we have is to drop into the rapids and use the driftwood to float."

"You serious?" Gene asked, before he was interrupted.

"Ga-Ga-Guys. I c-can't hold on m-much longer…" Edgar yelled from above as his grip weakened.

Jack looked up. "Stay strong, Edgar. You can do it." But seconds later, the bridge slipped out of Edgar's grasp and Jack and Gene plunged, until—

"Oooh-aaa ooo-yaa!" Jack and Gene reared their heads back. A man was flying across the sky on what looked like a rope swing.

"It's Tarzan!" Jack hollered.

The man on the rope swing flew full speed at Jack, Gene, and the deer. He kicked his feet out to the side with one arm holding the rope, and he reached out with his other arm. With one full scoop, he grabbed all three.

"Whoaah! What the … " Jack yelled.

"Stay still!" the man said. He kicked his legs out, building momentum to fly back toward Edgar and the safety of land. He flew over the river. He was headed straight for the face of the jagged rock ledge underneath Edgar. The three flew upward toward land but were still heading toward the cliff face. Moments before the collision, the man kicked to the side, and let go of the rope.

"We're gonna die!" Jack screamed, free-falling, looking down between his feet while the view changed from rapids, to ledge, to…

Bang. Bang. Bang.

Jack, Gene, and the deer met the ground with a thud. The man landed gracefully on his feet.

For several minutes, all the Bandits could do was lay there, winded. Their chests and abdomens expanded and retracted while they caught their breath.

Jack was about to call out to the man, but he vanished. Just like that, as quickly as he appeared out of the blue, he was gone.

Meanwhile, the deer untangled its antlers from Gene's underwear and walked gingerly away, favoring one of its hind legs. It stumbled before it turned to them, put its tongue in the air, and made a soft, gentle noise. *Wee.*

"Wow. I think he's thanking us," Jack said.

"Thank you," Gene called. "You saved my life."

Jack, Gene, and Edgar, feet away, locked eyes and, without a word needing to be said, busted up into deep belly laughter.

"Ha ha ha ha…" They cried tears of joy and relief.

Jack summarized the events, while fighting through constant laughing fits. "And—ha—his underwear… ha ha… right on his antlers. Oh, my god. Ha ha ha… Oh, man, my cheeks hurt from laughing, but probably not as bad as yours."

Gene smiled at Jack's underwear jokes. Ordinarily he would be annoyed, but this time he was more thankful to be alive.

The three went quiet and huddled up. They noticed the man reappear in the distance.

"There he is," Jack said. The man was stretching in the grass as though nothing had ever happened.

"Whoa! What do you think, guys?" Jack whispered.

"He looks like that actor I was talking about before. What's his name? Johnny something?" Gene asked.

"D-Depp," Edgar said with a smile. "It-It's J-Johnny D-Depp."

"Dude, where were you when we were trying to come up with his name a while ago?" Jack asked.

"Ha ha," Edgar awkwardly laughed.

"Well, what do you think? Is it him?" Gene asked.

The Bandits scanned the tall, lean-muscled, long-haired, and unshaven man.

"He kind of looks like him a little bit. And he looks like he's doing yoga; that's like a Hollywood thing to do," Jack said. "But I don't know. His cheekbones and skin are a bit too prominent and weathered."

"Yeah, but that's the thing these days," Gene said. "As contradictory as this sounds, girls like a guy who's rugged, a little bit ugly, yet handsome."

"I somehow feel you, man. Girls like complex things," Jack agreed.

"Amen to that," Gene said, bumping Jack's fist. Seconds after, they noticed the man looking at them.

"Gene—come on, man, go talk to him." Jack tried to push the burden on Gene.

"No, you go talk to him," Gene said, with a nudge to Jack's shoulder.

Gene and Jack argued over who was going to talk to him. Like usual, it ended with Gene conceding. "I'll go do it."

Jack beamed with excitement and asked, "Well, what are you going to say to him? 'Thank you'? 'Are you Johnny Depp?' 'Why have you been standing here like a statue for almost twenty minutes without saying a word?' Actually, now that I'm thinking about it, that's kind of creepy, you know?"

Gene scratched his chin. "I know. I'll just go up to him and say thank you. And I'll get really close and try to smell his breath. If it smells like wine or rum, then we probably know it's Johnny Depp, right?"

Jack and Edgar exchanged shoulder shrugs. "Don't jump to conclusions, man. Just say thanks," Jack urged.

Gene walked up to the man.

The man stood but didn't say a word. He was shirtless and wearing torn jeans. Gene rubbed his nose as the man's bad earthy smell reached his nostrils.

His eyes came up to the man's chest. Gene adjusted and looked up at his face. Then he looked back at Jack and Edgar, who stood like they had been frozen in time. The man stared into Gene's eyes, making him feel even more uncomfortable and maybe even scared. Gene shook the feelings away. He pulled himself up to his full height and said, "Thank you. You saved our lives."

The man remained silent. He looked at Jack and Edgar, then down to Gene, before breaking a big smile with a mix of crooked, yellow, and missing teeth.

"That's all right," he said. "My name's Lito. Pleased to meet ya." He put out a strong, weathered, and bony hand. Gene shook it and noticed the strength of Lito's hands, while at the same time feeling the gentleness his handshake possessed.

Gene looked back at the Bandits, before saying, "Excuse me one moment."

Gene walked back to Jack and Edgar.

"Okay, guys." Gene made a throat slashing gesture. "Those teeth, no way they're cutting it in Hollywood. Not a chance. So even if he's playing a character named Lito, it's not him."

"Did you smell any wine or rum on his breath?" Jack asked.

Gene shook his head. "Not a single whiff. Only thing I could smell was bad breath and maybe some B.O. No wine or rum."

Jack and Edgar nodded and looked toward Lito.

"Honestly," Gene continued, "he seems pretty nice, even though he looks a little bit scruffy. I bet he knows this area like the back of his hand. I think we should show him the map so he can help us find the gold."

"No way, Gene. Not a chance," Jack snapped. "Do not say a single word about the map to him. You guys hear? We are just in the woods going for a little hike if he asks."

Their conversation was suddenly halted by Lito calling out, "Hey, guys. Y'all want somethin' to eat or drink? Y'all can check out my camp. It's about a quarter mile downstream."

The Bandits looked at each other as they pondered what they should do. Was he a hero? A genuine guy who was homeless and lived in the woods? A criminal hiding from the law? A serial killer? Hmmm... So many possibilities.

Chapter 13
Life's a Tightrope

The Boonetown Bandits huddled up. Gene, for once, took charge.

"All right, guys, I say we have a vote. The majority wins." The three agreed. "Edgar, you first. What do you say?"

"Y-Yes." Edgar made his decision quickly.

Gene continued. "Jack, what about you?"

"Dude, he looks like a crazy homeless guy. Maybe even a possible serial killer. I say no. Like capital N-O. NO."

"Yeah, Jack, you're probably right." Gene nodded his head. "But I don't know. Something tells me I want to take a chance for once, so... Well, I say yes."

Gene turned his head toward Lito and shouted, "Okay, Lito, we're coming!"

The Bandits moved slowly toward Lito. Jack, who was normally so brave and a bit cocky, was surprised at how nervous he felt.

"Hey," Jack said. He pointed at Edgar. "This is Edgar."

Lito smiled toward Edgar.

Jack pulled Gene in front of him. "You already met—sort of met Gene, and my name is Jack."

"Pleased to meet ya," Lito said. "Follow me. This way."

They followed behind Lito along the path that meandered next to the stream. Up in the distance, they saw a cleared-out section of brush with some planks and grayish-white sycamores, and what looked like a tightrope tied from one tree to another. The Bandits scanned the area for any clues that this might be a killer or someone from one of those real crime shows on TV. As they walked close to Lito's camp, more things came into view. They saw a rope with a tire hanging over the water; a clothesline with shorts, shirts, and underwear hanging off of it; an old couch; an interesting teepee-looking building; a table; and a big pot and pan.

Chills and goosebumps shot through Gene's body. He could barely swallow, noticing something on the old table between a pan and a covered dish.

"Jack," Gene whispered. "Look."

Jack looked to where Gene was pointing, about twenty feet in front of where Lito was leading them. He gagged. "What the…"

Jack and Gene motioned to each other. "What should we do?" Jack asked. Beads of sweat multiplied on Edgar's forehead, and he grew even more docile. Fear overtook them. "He probably wants us alive, because we'll taste better," Jack said, panicked.

"Should we run? Attack him? Stay?" Jack whispered.

Jack knelt and picked up three baseball-sized rocks. He gave one to Gene and Edgar. They were ready to knock Lito out before he could pick up the sharp, bloody knife on the table. Their hearts beat out of their chests as Lito moved closer to the table. Like a SWAT team general, Jack motioned the Bandits. They sneaked closer to him.

Jack whispered, "He's a crazy killer. Let's knock him out with the rocks. After we do, Edgar, you're going to sit on him." Edgar nodded back at Jack. "On the count of three, hit him in the head." Gene nodded. "One, two, and…"

All of a sudden, Lito faced them, a knife pointing at them in one hand and something in the other hand.

"Aagh!" the Bandits screamed, frozen like statues. *Is it a head from the last victim?* Jack thought.

"Y'all hungry?" Lito stretched out his other hand. "Want some strawberry rhubarb pie?" He held out the knife. "Try a lick from the knife if ya want. It's my grandma's recipe."

The Boonetown Bandits dropped their rocks and let out a deep sigh of relief. They burst into laughter.

"What's so funny?" Lito asked.

"Nothing," Jack said.

"Y-Yeah," Edgar said. "W-We're just glad you s-s-saved us."

"Glad to be of service. Now how about that pie?"

"Oh, wow! That does look good," Jack said. "I'm actually not sure I've ever even had rhubarb pie."

"Oh, yeah, I'd have to say this is one of the best y'all will ever taste," Lito said. "All the ingredients are fresh from the garden over there." Lito pointed to a garden in the meadow. It was lush with vegetables and strawberries.

"I'll try some," Jack said.

"Edgar and I will take some, too," Gene said, before curiously inquiring, "I do have to ask you, how do you bake a pie out here?"

"Look over there." Lito pointed at the small, tarp-covered, stick-built teepee building with a metal chimney sticking out of the middle. "That's my house. It's called a yurt. That's where I sleep."

"Oh, a yurt?" Gene said. "You know, yurts were invented in…"

"We know what a yurt is, and we don't care when they were invented," Jack interrupted.

Lito chuckled this time. "Anyway, you see in the middle there? That's a wood stove. And I'll tell ya what, it takes a bit, but you can get the temperature just right for baking. Just like my grandma used to make."

Lito patted his stomach. "So don't be shy, take a bite. Tell me what ya think."

The Bandits and Lito sat on the tall chairs around the table, and the four looked over the crisp, golden crust baked to perfection. Breathing in the smell and aroma of sweet strawberry, they pushed their forks through the flakey crust into the strawberries and rhubarb and watched the strawberry ooze out the sides.

"Wow," Jack said. "This is really good."

"Amazing," Gene agreed.

"G-Good." Edgar smiled, with strawberry on his lips.

Lito clapped his hands. "I knew y'all would like it. Now, remember, there is always more to go around."

Whether Lito meant it or not, the boys took him at his word, devouring the whole pie.

"Oh, man, I'm full…" Jack rubbed his belly.

"Second that," Gene said.

Edgar held up two thumbs.

Lito directed the boys to make themselves at home on the couch. They made themselves comfy, and Lito asked, "So what brings y'all here?"

Gene and Edgar looked directly at Jack.

"Why are you guys looking at me?" Jack said, in a joking manner.

Lito looked into Jack's eyes. "I take it you're kind of the leader of this little group."

Jack smiled. He liked being thought of as the leader. "Well, here's the thing: we just wanted to hike and camp out."

"Well, that's fun. Kids need to do that more nowadays. When we were kids, we used to spend all our time outside. We would be outside all day long. Now kids never go out. Video games, cell phones. Seems they need a device for everything."

Jack glanced at Gene and said, "Yeah. I do agree. What do you think, Gene?"

Gene glanced back at Jack and said, "I think you owe me money when we get back."

Lito laughed. "Well, boys, I can tell y'all are getting restless. Why don't you look around and explore a bit? I got a tire swing you can sit on, a canoe, a kayak, and even a tightrope if y'all want."

"So… which way to the tightrope?" Jack remembered how walking over the tree trunk was kind of like walking a tightrope.

Lito laughed. "Now that's the spirit, Jack." He patted him on the back.

The Bandits and Lito made their way away from the river toward the tightrope in the meadow. It was strung between two sycamore trees. En route, Jack noticed a sapling that looked like it had been in a fight.

"Whoa, what did that?" Jack asked, as the other three huddled around the tree.

Lito smiled. "You don't know what that is?"

The Bandits looked at each other.

"I guess if y'all kids don't have a cell phone app for it, you probably don't know, do you?"

Gene chimed in. "It's a buck rub. They usually do this to get the velvet off their horns. Science class is all coming back to me."

"Leave it to you to know all about deer antlers," Jack joked. "Antlers can also be a real pain in the butt. Right, Gene?"

The four laughed.

"Good one, Jack," Lito said. "I guess books can teach you some things, but now you can truly touch it, see it, and connect with it."

Soon they reached the tightrope stretched between two sycamores.

"Here we are. It's twenty feet up. I built the platforms on each side myself. Pretty nice, huh?"

"Sure is." Jack admired.

"So, well, y'all want me to teach you how to do it?"

The Bandits looked at each other, and eagerly answered, "Yes."

Lito jumped onto one of the ladders and climbed atop the platform. "Now, here's the thing about this here tightrope. How y'all feelin'? That pie sitting, okay? You sure ate a lot."

The Bandits shrugged. "Good, we guess."

Lito laughed. "Good, you guess? Well, let me tell you something. When you feel good, you guess, you ain't living or feeling good." Lito walked onto the tightrope. "But when you're up here, you're alive." Lito walked across gracefully.

When he reached the other side, he called down, "Walking on a tightrope teaches you about life."

Gene called up to him. "Aren't you afraid to fall?"

Lito stopped and looked down. "Fall? Fall? That ain't even in my vocabulary. See, fallin' is a problem. When I walk across here, if I go one way too much, I counterbalance, and that becomes the solution." The

Bandits listened intently. "See, it don't matter how much you struggle or flail your arms. As long as you keep your eye on the prize and keep your feet one in front of the other, you'll be fine. You can either dwell on problems, like falling, or you can find solutions. It's as simple as that."

Jack chimed in. "Well, what's the trick?"

Lito chuckled. "Well, Jack, you know what it is?"

Jack fired back. "Um... No. But you have a habit of asking questions back." The Bandits laughed. "No, that's why I'm asking you, man."

"All you have to do is believe. Well, and maybe a lil' practice!" Lito laughed. "You see where you wanna end up, and feel the feelin' of being there, then you just take one step at a time until you reach it." Lito walked across the rope until he was just a few feet away from the other platform. "It's really that simple." Lito stepped onto the platform. "So, which of y'all want to try it next?"

Jack's hand shot straight up like a bullet. "I do."

Lito motioned Jack to come up. Jack climbed onto the platform. Lito gave Jack a long balancing stick. It was like a pool cue, only longer and looked like it had been made from a maple tree.

"All right, Jack, give it a whirl."

Jack's hands shook, and his palms sweat.

"Well... what do I do? Do you have any tips?"

"Just take a deep breath, get your mind right, see and feel yourself reachin' the other platform, and then when you get it, just head out. One step at a time. Remember, you have to believe. If you lose your balance, find the solution."

"Well, that's all fine and dandy, but do you have a net in case I fall? Or can you go down and catch me?"

Lito looked at Jack. "Well, I guess, but if that's the case, you sure ain't believin'. I think that's a recipe for a fall, Jack."

Maybe I can do this? Jack thought. Then he called out, "All right, here goes nothing." Jack stepped onto the rope. "Whoa…" His feet and ankles shook. His arms and hips swayed in opposing directions. Every part of his being shook as he tried to keep upright.

"Keep firm, Jack. Find the solution. Believe." Lito's words echoed in the background.

Taking three more confident steps, Jack's legs began to shake uncontrollably. His calves spasmed. His balance began to go…

"Ugh! Ugh!" Jack screamed, flailing his arms.

Chapter 14
Lito's Story

Gene and Edgar anxiously yelled to Jack, "Grab the rope! Grab the rope!"

"Believe, Jack," Lito called from the platform. "Feel it in every inch of your bones. Find the solution."

Tightening his core and shifting his weight, Jack regained his center of gravity before taking a step, and then another. Building momentum, he moved along the rope. Jack stopped and looked down at the ground.

"Just take one step at a time," Lito called.

Once again, Jack's legs shook. He lost his focus and balance. His arms swayed. He released the balance stick, his calves quivered, and he began to fall. "Aaah!"

"Got ya." Lito quickly lunged over and grabbed onto Jack's shirt, and carried him back to the platform.

"Oh, man. Phew..." Jack said, winded and scared, as Lito held on to him. "I believed, Lito. I truly did."

"You did a good job, Jack. But you know where you went wrong?"

Jack smiled. "When I looked at the ground, I think."

Lito and Jack climbed down to the grassy ground.

"You're exactly right, Jack. You stopped takin' one step at a time. And with that, you stopped believin'. But it was a heck of a try! If you ain't trying somethin' harder than you can do, then you ain't ever gonna learn."

Lito looked at Edgar and Gene. "All right, y'all wanna try?"

Gene and Edgar made eye contact before Edgar shook his head, and Gene politely said, "We're good."

"To be honest, Lito," Jack said. "We probably need to get going soon so we can set up camp for the night."

"Actually, before we go," Gene said. "I was wondering... why are you here, Lito?"

Lito cracked a smile. "All of this. Just look at it; it's beautiful. Utterly beautiful. Nature just speaks to me. It's everything my heart desires. I feel I'm the richest man in the world."

Jack, Gene, and Edgar looked around.

Not quite seeing the same reality, Jack asked, "Not to be rude, but if you're the richest man in the world, why do you choose to live in a yurt by the river? Why don't you have a Ferrari or a Lambo?"

Lito chuckled. "Well, I've been around a lot, Jack, and seen a lotta things. I grew up here. Played in that river." Lito pointed to the water. "Lived here till I was eight, before I moved to Birmingham. Well, my parents passed away in a car accident, and so, I moved with my grandma. Then she died a few years later, and so there I was, left to fend for myself."

Gene shifted his feet. "Ah, sorry, man."

Lito waved them toward the camp. They followed him and sat by the fire.

"So, I joined the circus," Lito said. "I was an acrobat. Toured the country, even toured the world. Even met my wife, Monica, on tour."

Jack looked around. "Wife? Is she here?"

Lito didn't answer. "Then one day," he said, "I got an opportunity to buy that circus, and I did. So, we toured nonstop, and I saw a lotta places and did a lotta things. But that one day in February in Albuquerque changed my life forever. Monica was a trapeze artist. I kissed her like I did every night and I said, 'You go on and give 'em a show now.' Well, Monica lost her grip when she was on the trapeze that night and fell."

Lito paused. He choked up a bit. As tears rolled down his weathered face, Lito continued with a vulnerable twinge in his voice. "I went and rushed on over to her. Told her she was the love of my life. We held hands in the ambulance until the good Lord took her."

Tears poured from Lito's eyes, running off the etched lines of his face. He looked up to the sky. Jack, Gene, and Edgar walked over to Lito. They patted his back.

"I'm so sorry to hear," Gene said.

Lito composed himself and stood.

"Thanks. I really appreciate it. Well, anyway, so I sold that circus the next day. The money that I got I gave to charity and kept some to live off of. Don't wanna sound like a big shot or nothin', but I could have bought four Ferraris with the money I sold the circus for, but it wouldn't have changed how I felt."

"Guess so," Jack said. "But I would've bought at least one Ferrari."

Lito chuckled. "So, I took the train and got a job in Missoula, Montana. Beautiful country and beautiful rivers. Worked part-time at a grocery store, then I decided to start makin' my way back here. I went from Casper, Wyoming, to Omaha, Nebraska, then spent some time in Kansas City, Missouri." He poked at the fire with a stick. "Every stop was an experience. And I always did enough to make ends meet. But when I got here to the Great Gauley, I knew I was finally home again."

Jack asked, "Why's this place so special, compared to everywhere else?"

Lito looked him in the eye. "Because it's home, Jack. But I had to leave and go away to truly see it with the eyes I see today. If I would have stayed here, it would just be all I know. I wouldn't see the eagles flying free, or the limestone and sandstone walls jettin' out of the water with the same appreciation. I wouldn't appreciate the birds and the plant life that's unique here."

"Wow," Edgar said. "S-Sounds n-nice."

Lito continued. "The point is, when it's time for y'all to leave, go spread your wings, go explore, and when you come back, you'll find that you're a different person. And you might just appreciate where you came from. But, then again, that's my truth, but it may not be yours. Anyways, enough of me ramblin' on."

"No, Lito. We hear you. You didn't ramble on that long," Jack said. "And thanks again for saving our lives."

The Bandits and Lito exchanged hugs and goodbyes.

"Y'all be safe, you hear?" Lito yelled as they walked away. "You know where I'll be if ya need me."

The Bandits walked off to set up camp for the night. Jack pulled the map from his bag.

"All right. Let's go southeast about a half mile to set up for the night. This should get us to the treasure by tomorrow evening if all goes as planned."

"Are you sure you don't want to show Lito the map, Jack?" Gene asked.

Jack stopped walking and faced Gene and Edgar. "I think we can do this on our own. This is our journey. We can do this on our own."

Gene shook his head. The sun began to tuck itself under the trees. Dusk would be coming on shortly, so they pressed on to set up camp before nightfall.

Chapter 15
First Night Fight

The boys set up their camp for the night in a small clearing they discovered after an hour's hike through the woods. They found tree stumps to use as seats and river mud-caked plywood to put on top of two stumps for a table. Gene and Edgar set off into the woods for firewood.

While they were gone, Jack created a Boy-Scout teepee in the firepit with some of the small kindling around the site. He grabbed a lighter from his pack, dried orange peels from a Ziploc bag, and an old newspaper from his bag to ignite the process. After a few failed flicks, a thumb blister, and a shake of the lighter, the spark finally ignited.

Gene and Edgar returned with arms filled with wood and were greeted by the smell of burnt wood and the sight of a small, orange-lit kindling fire. Gene and Edgar put down their thicker pieces of wood.

"Come on, Edgar," Gene said. "Let's go find some smaller limbs to break and add to the fire."

Jack joined the search and, as Jack always did, he took things to the next level. "Check this out, guys. I'm Bruce Lee."

Jack dashed straight at a tree and attempted a flip-spin kick through the limb he set up along the table. But he bounced straight off the tree. He fell on his butt and chuckled. "Maybe I'm more like Bruised Lee."

"Wow, man. Yeah, you probably shouldn't try that anymore." Gene smiled and winked at Jack. "I would stick to maybe a simple 101 karate kick. Or maybe just do this." Gene broke the limb over his knee and threw it into the fire.

The Bandits sat around the roaring fire, roasting marshmallows, eating s'mores, laughing, and giggling as flickers of light reflected on their faces.

"All right, but seriously, don't you think Sarah and I would be the perfect couple?" Jack said, licking the chocolate off his fingers. "I mean, I know what she likes. Her favorite color is green. She loves mint chocolate chip ice cream. She likes to wear pastels. She probably secretly loves me."

Laughter. Gene and Edgar both shot s'mores out of their mouths into the fire. Belly laughter continued. Edgar snorted and a marshmallow went down the wrong pipe. Edgar coughed and laughed simultaneously.

"What's so funny?" Jack asked, holding out his hands.

"You're delusional." Gene tried to hold back his laughter. "She's sure keeping it a secret, all right. So secret, in fact, that she doesn't even know!" *Laughter.*

"Wow, guys," Jack said. He was always surprisingly mature and serious when discussing Sarah. "Am I a big joke to you?"."

Edgar and Gene composed themselves. Gene cleared his throat.

"Cool," Gene said. "But here's the reason you guys don't fit. She doesn't like you, man. She thinks you love yourself. Wait... She *knows* you love yourself." Gene and Edgar busted out in laughter.

"Well, what's not to love? I mean, I'm funny, adventurous, spontaneous... What else am I?" Jack asked.

Gene responded. "Oh, that you are. That you are, Jack. But you love yourself a little too much. You're kind of conceited."

"Okay, okay, Gene," Jack said. "Let's not focus on me." Jack turned to Edgar. "So, who do you like, Edgar?"

Edgar gave a blank look and shuffled his feet. He knew he was supposed to like someone; at least other boys in school did. But he really wasn't sure and didn't want to open himself up to anything either.

"A-A-All of 'em!" Edgar said the first thing to come to his mind.

"Olive Umm?" Jack joked. "Never heard of her."

"All right, new subject! Too much girl talk!" Gene said.

As the sun set behind the tall trees, the Bandits stared into the fire and tried to keep things light. Occasionally one or the other, or sometimes all three,

113

yawned. It had, after all, been a very long day. Jack felt especially tired, but he was not going to be the first to say so.

They talked about Lito and school and parents, but mostly they just stared into the fire and munched down goodies they'd packed from home.

Jack looked over to Gene, who seemed to be deep in thought. Jack thought maybe he had been thinking about all the times Jack was kind of a jerk and said, "You know, I'm impressed you knew that was a buck rub today."

Gene nodded. "Yeah, thanks. No big deal."

Jack poked the fire with a stick. "Hey, Gene, how long have we been friends?"

Gene looked directly at him. "What do you want?" The firelight gave Gene's face a stern appearance.

"Chill, Gene," Jack said.

"No, man. What do you want, Jack?" Gene shouted and carefully inspected his s'more, making sure Jack didn't pull a prank. "Why are you sucking up to me, Jack? Anytime you're extra nice, it's either because you want something, or you have something up your sleeve."

"That's not true," Jack said.

Gene's face lit up in the firelight. "Hmmm. Well, let's see. How about the time you were so nice and let me have a couple slices of your mom's pepperoni pizza? And you kept asking me if I liked it and to eat up because I looked malnourished," Gene said, wide-eyed and staring directly into Jack's eyes. "Then, when I took the next bite, you busted up laughing, as my mouth exploded and

114

caught fire because you put 100x super-hot sauce under the pepperoni."

Jack tried not to laugh. "Oh, wow! I completely forgot about that. Yeah, so okay, like one time I did that."

Gene shook his head. "Well, then I remember vividly you gave me a glass of milk to cool off the burn. Then I find myself chewing the milk, not drinking it, because it was so curdled."

Jack shook his head. "Okay, okay. That was one day. Big deal."

Edgar made a funny face. "Y-Yuck. M-Makes me want to p-puke just th-thinking about it."

Gene poked the fire with a stick. "It's just stuff like that, Jack, that you do that really starts to get old."

"Hey, man. Friends are supposed to tease each other and play little jokes. If I didn't do that, it would mean I probably don't like you. Just look at Edgar. I joke a little with him, too."

Gene shouted. "Listen. You can be a jerk sometimes. You're selfish, arrogant, and judgmental. It's no wonder Sarah doesn't like you. And stop putting down my friend Edgar."

Edgar stood like an awakened giant. "S-S-Stop, G-Gene. J-Jack m-may be a j-jerk at t-times. B-B-But what y-you d-do is even worse."

"What did I do, Edgar?" Gene asked.

Edgar looked Gene straight in the eye. "W-Well, y-y-you c-come over to my house all the t-time. Then w-when I s-see you in school, you d-don't even a-a-

115

acknowledge me." Tears rolled down Edgar's puffy cheeks.

"Wait. You go over to Edgar's house a lot, Gene?" Jack asked. "Why didn't you tell me the truth? You just said your sister had a dance recital like a gazillion times. I wouldn't have teased you about it."

"You would have teased me, and you know it, Jack!" Gene yelled as his eyes welled up.

"Who c-cares, G-Gene? D-Does it matter? J-Just because I st-st-stutter, doesn't m-mean I'm s-stupid. It also d-doesn't mean I d-don't have f-f-feelings," Edgar said.

Gene put his head in his hands. Tears flooded down his cheeks. Jack stared blankly into the fire, realizing they were at their breaking point.

Edgar stood, sobbing. He grabbed his duffel bag and walked off into the darkness.

Chapter 16
Bandit Breakup?

Jack walked toward the river while his mind raced about the fight. It wasn't their first argument. He thought about how it was true that he liked to play jokes on Gene, but it was always in good fun. He kicked a stone into the water. *Guess I didn't know it bothered him so much.*

Jack picked up another rock and tossed it into the water. *I better make this right.* If Gene left, they might never find the treasure. Jack knew he needed Gene, and not just for the treasure, but as his friend.

Jack bent down, looked in the water, and stared at his reflection with the light of the moon in the background.

"You can be a real jerk, you know that?" he said to himself. "No wonder Sarah doesn't like you." Jack put his head into his hands and held back tears. "Why do I always have to be Mr. Know-It-All? Always have to one-up everyone. I guess the joke's on me this time." Jack wiped his nose on his sweatshirt sleeve and kicked the dirt. "What's my problem? Seriously, what's my—" Jack looked out over the water. He took a deep breath of summer air. He remembered what Lito had told him.

"Wait. What's my solution? Oh, yeah. What's my solution?"

Suddenly the obvious dawned on him. They needed to find Edgar and talk things out. Jack sprinted up the bank for the campsite. When he got there, winded, he looked around, calling, "Gene... Gene? Where are you, bud?" He noticed Gene's backpack was gone. He heard a noise in the distance. Jack sprinted toward the sound. He plowed through the sappy cypress trees and barreled through the jaggers. "Ugh, crap," he yelled, scurrying up the bank where he heard Gene screaming at Edgar.

The sound grew louder and closer. "No, don't, Edgar. No!" Gene cried.

Jack rushed in between the two. The light of the moon illuminated the clearing and the Bandits. Gene looked like he'd just seen a ghost. Jack noticed Edgar sobbing and asked, "What jaggers did you hit, Edgar? You're bleeding..."

Edgar didn't respond. He just stood there, sobbing.

Gene put his hand on Edgar's arm. "He just kept running right into the thorn bushes. Cut himself up pretty bad."

Jack crumpled on the inside. He felt so responsible for what had happened. "I'm sorry, Edgar."

Gene yelled at Jack, "You can be such an arrogant jerk sometimes."

Jack approached Edgar, but Edgar backed up. "Edgar, we love you, man. You're a good-hearted friend."

118

Gene pushed Jack aside. "Edgar, I'm sorry. I never thought about how you felt. Honestly, you're one of my best friends. I'm so sorry. I should've stuck up for you all those times."

Minutes passed, and Edgar, red and enraged, started to relax and calm down.

"Just keep breathing deep," Jack said. "We promise to never ignore you again."

Gene hugged Edgar.

Jack took off his shirt. "Here, Edgar, let me wipe some of the dirt and blood off you, man." Jack wrapped his shirt tightly around his wrist, wiping Edgar's scratched forehead and arms. "All right. Looking much better now."

The Bandits put their arms around each other.

"All right, Edgar," Jack said, looking into his eyes. "I'll promise you this. I'll never tease you, and you're always welcome at my lunch table from here on out, but you have to promise not to run away anymore, okay, bud?"

Edgar smiled and said, "Pr-Pr-Promise, J-Jack?"

"Promise," Jack said.

"You can even sit at the less popular end of the table with me," Gene said. "You're my friend, and I want the whole school to know."

Exhausted, the three sat in the dirt, overtaken with the day and emotion. Within minutes, all were horizontal and sound asleep on the comfy dirt mattress that nature had provided them, with only the evergreens as shelter.

Chapter 17
Another Stranger on the Trail

Gene woke to the sound of birds chirping and the smell of summer dew on the grass and pines. He yawned and stretched, and then stretched again, making certain his reach did not miss Jack.

Jack's body jolted before he lifted his head, sporting a rooster hairstyle from his cowlick.

"Gene? What the heck are you doing here? Actually, what am I doing here? Where are we?"

Gene laughed. "We're in the woods, looking for the treasure, right?"

"Yeah, yeah. I'm not a big morning person, you know that." Jack stood and stretched. "I'm hungry. We can share those muffins you brought if you want?"

"Oh, can we share my blueberry muffins? I'm glad you're so giving, Jack," Gene joked.

Jack looked at Edgar, still asleep. "I feel awful about treating Edgar the way I did. Poor guy."

Gene nodded. "Yeah, he can't control the stutter all the time. Not his fault."

Jack's face turned stern. "Well, I meant what I said yesterday. I'll never make fun of him again. I'm serious."

Edgar's body shuffled like a caterpillar in a cocoon before finally waking. Springing up, Edgar smiled and said, "M-Morning, Gene."

Gene smiled back. "Hey, Edgar. How you feeling?"

Edgar shook his head, "D-Did you g-guys m-m-mean that?"

"Mean what, Edgar?" Jack asked.

"Y-You'll s-sit with me n-next year?" Edgar asked.

Gene laughed. "Yes, Edgar. You're one of us now. We're the Boonetown Bandits." Gene and Edgar bumped fists.

"That's right, man. The Three Musketeers," Jack said.

Edgar laughed. "I th-th-thought we were the B-Boonetown Bandits."

They all laughed and shared pats on the shoulders. The Bandits were back in business.

After a quick breakfast of blueberry muffins, granola, and soda to wash it all down, they decided to get back to treasure hunting.

Jack waved the map in the air. "Come here, guys. So, I scouted it out. If we put in a good hike today, I think we can get to the treasure by this evening. And I'm giving us some leeway time, too."

The boys all looked over the map as Jack pointed out the trail.

"But what is that, right at the end?" Gene asked.

"Hmmm… That's Shotgun Falls, I believe, and the treasure is right there beside it." Jack tapped the map.

"How are we going to get to it, Jack?" Gene asked. "I mean, I can't really tell because this isn't a topographic map, but the drawing sort of shows, like, huge cliffs on both sides and what looks like massive waterfalls and rapids to me."

"Y-Yeah," Edgar said. "It l-looks kind of tr-treacherous."

"Gene, you're such a worrier. You worry about everything. Besides, that Thomas Hubbs guy was probably just all stressed out about getting burned anyways. He might not have thought things through."

"Not thought things through, huh? Like us?" Gene said. "We didn't think about bringing a boat on a whitewater adventure. That's like forgetting skis to go skiing. That's kind of a pretty big thing we missed."

"We'll make it work, Gene. Anyone who ever accomplished anything didn't know how they were going to do it. They just did it. We'll figure it out as we go." Jack folded the map.

The Bandits hitched their packs onto their shoulders and set out along the riverside path for what they were sure would be a great day of adventure.

They had been trudging along the riverside for close to an hour when Jack stopped and pulled the map from his backpack.

"All right, guys. We're right here." Jack pointed on the map. "We need to keep following this path southeast, and then we'll have to cross the river at some point."

Gene took a closer look. "Actually, Jack, if we keep going along the creek, in about a half mile we can probably cross right here." Gene pointed to the widest spot of the river on the map.

"It looks kind of like a pool, and usually that means it could be deep but calm water. We might be able to swim there and cool off."

"You know what, Gene?" Jack said, with a smile.

"What, Jack?" Gene asked.

"Times just like this make me realize why we're friends." The boys bumped fists, making sure Edgar got in on the appreciation.

"Well, Jack, when I feel that way about you, I'll say the same." Gene laughed and walked down the trail with Edgar.

"Funny. Funny, Mr. Smarty-pants!" Jack yelled, as he jogged to catch up.

The Bandits wandered down the trail. The trail ran right beside the river. They admired the beautiful riffs, ripples, and pocket water the Great Gauley had to offer. The sweet aroma of summer filled the air with the honeysuckles, pines, and the smell of the spring water spritzing up from the rapids.

As they continued on the trail, they came across a kayaker taking a break on the side of the river. The man, decked out in a wet suit, closely resembled an astronaut without the full-faced helmet.

"Hello!" the man called.

Jack, of course, went full speed ahead. "Hey. That's a cool kayak, man," Jack said.

"Thanks. Yeah, it's a Jackson. I take my kayaking pretty seriously." The kayaker laughed.

"Rapids look pretty huge in this river, huh?" Jack said.

"Ha ha, yeah. That may be an understatement. Well, at least when the CFS is up. It's running low now, so it makes it possible." The kayaker looked at Jack. "CFS, dude: cubic feet per second. Determines how the river is running."

"Yeah, cool," Jack said. "I know." He didn't.

The kayaker looked at Edgar. "Hey, dude, can you hand me the skirt sitting there?"

"Skirt?" Jack said. "You wear a skirt?"

Edgar gave the man an odd-looking contraption.

"Yeah," the kayaker said. He stepped into one end of the thing and pulled it up over his waist to just under his sternum. "You'll see. It keeps water out of the boat, and it even helps keep me in the boat. Name's Griffin, by the way."

"Oh, I'm Jack. Edgar is the one who gave you your skirt. And that's Gene."

Griffin stepped into the kayak and expertly pulled the bottom of the skirt around the opening of the cockpit. "There, see, now it's all snug, and the inside of the boat is waterproof."

"Cool," Jack said, "but you still wear a skirt."

The Bandits chuckled.

"Spray skirt," Griffin said.

Griffin was just about to push off when Jack asked, "Have you ever heard of Shotgun Falls?"

The kayaker turned the stern around to face them. "Yeah, lost a friend there. It's nothing to mess with. Each side of Shotgun Falls has huge cliffs, so there's no way to port around it either. You pretty much either drag your kayak back up the river to your car, or just run the rapids and hope you make it."

"Seriously?" Jack said.

"Yeah, man. Seriously. And there is also a storm coming this evening, so I'm getting off this river before I become a casualty. Have a safe trek and stay out of the river." Griffin raised his paddle to say goodbye and paddled away.

"Really, Jack?" Gene said, moving closer to him. "So, cliffs on each side and rapids that kill people? Sounds like fun. Glad you brought our climbing gear and our boat, and, oh, yeah, the paddle, too. But I'm sure we can just hope we 'make it,' right?"

"Gene... calm down," Jack said. "It'll all be okay. People make things out to be way bigger than they are. First off, Shotgun Falls isn't very far from here. And second, we can float. Humans are meant to float."

"You're not that stupid are you, Jack? I mean, come on. We float? Yeah, in a swimming pool, we'd float. In a river, we get thrown in the undertow, we drown, then someone finds us floating. So, you're right, we will float eventually, Jack."

"Gene, live a little. We'll find a spot to swim, cross the river, get some logs, and then we just float through the rapids to Shotgun Falls. We'll get the gold and just sneak off and walk to Chick-fil-A for dinner or something." Jack smiled, as the morning sun glinted in his eyes.

"I d-don't know," Edgar said. He picked up a stick and tossed it into the river. "M-M-Maybe this ain't s-s-such a good idea."

"Are you serious?" Jack asked. "Of course, it is. We'll find a way around the falls." He looked at Gene. "Somehow, right?"

Gene shrugged. "Let's get there first, and then we can decide."

"Well, I want that gold," Jack said. "Even if I have to go by myself."

Gene stepped toward Jack and punched his shoulder and smiled. "We won't make you go by yourself. So, let's get this show rolling!"

The Bandits set off on their quest, heading straight for Shotgun Falls. With each step they took, the midmorning sun got brighter and brighter and hotter and hotter. Their skin glistened as they pulled out their water bottles. They stopped in front of some ferns and squirted water into their mouths.

"Ughh, it's so hot," Jack said.

"Yeah, hand me that map," Gene said. "That swimming hole has to be getting close."

"I think it's really close, but here you go." Jack handed Gene the map. "Edgar, how you holding up, buddy?" Jack patted him on the back.

"H-Hot," Edgar said, out of breath. His face dripped sweat.

"Yeah, it's officially summer, and I'm officially ready to be in the water," Jack said.

"Oh, thank God!" Gene yelled, while pointing at the map. "It's maybe two hundred yards up this way." Gene pointed ahead on the trail.

The three ran down the trail, their packs bouncing on their backs. As they came closer to the swimming hole, the roar quieted, and the sight of the narrow, white, rushing river beautifully opened up into a big, calm pond of water. The water was nicely tucked between two jagged, gray limestone rock walls that made for very little current, yet nature's unselfishness allowed the river a ten-foot thruway between them to bless more things on its journey.

Edgar and Jack ran down the bank toward the water and kicked off their shoes. They stepped into the nice, cool spring-fed river. Fish, schools of them, darted through the gin-clear water under rock ledges and submerged trees. Shiny flashes of stripes—blues, chromes, violets—glistened.

Gene tucked his glasses into his backpack before he joined them.

"This feels amazing!" Jack yelled while he splashed his face with the refreshingly cool water.

The Bandits slowly waded out toward the middle of the river, where it was calm. They swam around, splashed, and laughed. Edgar floated on his back, with his shirt on, and kicked around, wearing a big smile on his face and looking into the blue sky. Gene swam cautiously, always the one on the lookout for danger.

Jack insisted on finding the deepest part of the river by diving down and pulling objects from the bottom. Gene and Edgar ignored him. They wanted no part of Jack's shenanigans.

But then…

Splash. Something torpedoed out of the water between them. It was Jack.

"Guys! Guys!" Jack gasped for air.

"Jeez, Jack. You scared us. Can't you just relax?" Gene said, annoyed.

"Guys… About ten feet down, there's a big rock," Jack said as he treads water.

"Yeah, Jack. Well, there are a lot of big rocks. We're in a river, you know?" Gene laughed.

"We should try to move it," Jack said.

"I'm not wasting energy on that," Gene said. "What's the point? Oh, wow, Jack!" Gene pointed to the other side. "Look at the cliff there?"

"Oh, man. Yes. I call jumping off it first," Jack yelled, his attention now drawn from the boulder.

Gene looked to Edgar and whispered, "Sure. Go for it." Edgar seconded it with a slight nod. "Actually, Jack, we have to go over there anyway, so why don't you scope it out, and Edgar and I will swim over and get the bags, okay?"

"Sounds good." Jack swam furiously to the other side.

Minutes passed, and Gene and Edgar almost finished the swim across the river with their bags over their heads. They were greeted by Jack standing on top of the fifty-foot cliff with both hands in the air.

"Check this out, guys!" Jack launched off into the air and performed a corkscrew flip and splashed into the water. Gene and Edgar put their hands up high as they rocked in the water, doing everything to keep the bags and map dry from the massive waves that followed.

"Oh, man. That was awesome," Jack yelled. "You guys have to try it."

Gene and Edgar touched the silt bottom with their toes and looked up at the cliff like it was the Empire State Building.

"Yeah. Hmm, probably going to pass on this one, too, Jack," Gene said.

"Aw, c'mon. You have to jump off of it," Jack said when he greeted them on the bank.

"I really don't think it's a prerequisite to find the treasure, Jack. This is not like pre-algebra for algebra. Two different things," Gene said.

"Okay, fine." Jack then looked at Edgar.

"Do you want to try?" Jack asked.

Edgar nodded, but it was clear he was nervous.

Jack and Gene studied the cliff face.

"Look," Jack said. "You can jump from that ledge. It's maybe ten feet to the water."

"I'll jump with you, Edgar," Gene said.

Edgar and Gene made their way up to the ledge.

"You know, a basketball rim is that height, right?" Jack called from the water. "Really nothing to worry about."

Jack's words deflected off of Gene as he curled his toes around the edge and looked down at the water and Jack, who was smiling ear to ear.

"Okay, here goes. Whoa!" Gene yelled, doing the running man through the air before he plunged into the water. As he cut through the surface, the bubbles tickled his face. He sprang off the bottom and broke the surface.

"Oh, wow!" Gene yelled, invigorated.

"Yeah, Gene!" Jack applauded. "All right, Edgar, it's your turn. Show us what you got," Jack encouraged.

"It's really fun, Edgar, nothing to worry about," Gene said.

Edgar took a deep breath. He stepped back from the ledge, looking afraid. Suddenly he took off his shirt and whipped it around over his head.

"Whooo! Yeah, Edgar!" Jack and Gene yelled.

"H-Here's t-to the s-s-summer of the B-Boonetown Bandits!" Edgar threw his shirt into the water and launched himself off the cliff. He broke through the water, and a massive wave followed. When he came to the surface, Edgar hollered, "Yeah!" His voice echoed between the cliffs.

Jack and Gene beamed with excitement for Edgar.

Jack put out his fists to congratulate both. "Here's to the best friends in the world. Bandits on three. One… two…"

"Bandits," they yelled.

The three laughed and swam around for a while until Jack asked, "So… what are you guys going to do with your share of the gold?"

"I don't know," Gene said. "But I'm thinking we should get moving, right?"

"What are you going to do with yours, Edgar?" Jack asked while he splashed his hands back and forth in the water.

"I'm g-going to b-buy my brother a new c-c-car and m-maybe s-some clothes," Edgar said.

"That would be cool. I'm going to buy a new bike frame, handlebars, new game…" Jack continued rambling off items.

Gene, followed by Edgar, swam to the riverbank, and climbed out of the water to dry off. Gene turned back and focused on something on top of the water behind Jack.

"Hey, Jack. There's—"

"Gene," Jack said. "Can't you see I'm talking here? I'm also going to buy my mom—"

"No, Jack," Gene cried. "Look behind—"

"Gene, you interrupt me one more time, and I'm dunking you in the water. Now, I'd probably buy Sarah…"

Edgar noticed the creature approaching Jack, who continued to splash water as he talked. Gene pulled out the *All About Nature* encyclopedia he'd packed and thumbed through the pages. He looked over the images of the snakes on the page, and the one lurking behind Jack. "Let me see, let me see… Copperheads can go in water, check. They have a diamond-shaped head; looks diamond enough, check. Has stripes, check." Gene looked toward Jack and yelled, "Oh, no, Jack!"

"I'm going to buy Mrs. Bombgardner a gift card to a salon, I'm going to buy…" Jack babbled on.

Looking on, Gene saw the snake was closing in on Jack, who kept splashing and yakking. Gene continued to read: "Stripes are wide on the side and narrow toward the backbone." He looked up. "No check. Refer to the next page for Northern Water Snake." Gene let out a big sigh as he flipped the page. "Has stripes that are narrow on the sides and wide on the backbone, check. Aggressive and will approach when threatened, check. Do not splash or they'll attack, no check."

Gene looked out toward Jack. He opened his mouth to holler, but it was too late.

"Agh!" Jack screamed.

Chapter 18
Spelunked

The water snake latched on to Jack's back. Spinning in circles, Jack flailed, doing anything he could to shake the snake off. He was like a cat chasing its tail, only in water.

"Gene! Edgar! Help! I'm gonna die!" Jack yelled, jumping up and down in the water. Gene and Edgar looked on, laughing, until they realized Jack really needed their help. The two scoured the ground for anything to help steer the snake away. They picked up small rocks and threw them at the snake. One rock soared in the air. Jack watched the rock in slow motion coming end over end over end over...

"Ow! What the hell are you guys doing?" Jack yelled, as he brought his hand to his forehead.

"Jack!" Gene yelled, motioning, "Wade to shore! Wade to shore!"

Jack splashed his hands and pulsated his body through the water. He screamed and tried to knock what he thought was an anaconda off his back. Finally, Jack made it to shore and stared at Edgar and Gene as he ran in place.

"What do we do?" Jack and Gene yelled in unison with their hands in the air.

"Okay, um…" Gene said, brainstorming out loud. "Okay, Jack, okay. Jack—spin around, spin around, Jack!" Gene said while frantically circling his hands. The snake was still clutched to Jack's back, and it looked like he had a long ponytail from the front view.

Jack danced in circles, but the snake still hung tight.

"Agh!" Edgar and Gene screamed while the Jack-snake-go-round narrowly clotheslined them multiple times.

"All right, all right!" Gene yelled, kneeling. "Edgar, this is stupid! Just duck. Jack, keep on spinning! Edgar, let's just back up so we don't have to keep ducking from the snake helicopter!"

"Come on! Do something, guys! I'm gonna fall over!" Jack screamed.

"All right. Edgar, you're going to tackle Jack from the side, and when you do, I'll grab the snake and hopefully fling it off of him! Sound like a plan?"

"P-Plan!" Edgar nodded.

"All right. One, two, three… Go!"

Sprinting like a linebacker to a quarterback, Edgar landed a bone-crunching hit on Jack that would make any NFL football player proud. Bouncing off the ground, Jack's mouth filled with dirt as a cloud of dust followed. Gene wasted no time and jumped on Jack's back. He grabbed the snake's tail with both hands and pulled and tugged with all his might. The snake stretched like a rubber band until, suddenly, the snake released its bite and swiveled its head around. Gene and the snake's beady eyes locked for a moment. The snake's forked tongue flickered, it recoiled, and lunged directly at Gene's glasses.

"Agh!" Gene screamed as his glasses steamed up, and his face quickly turned pale. Gene catapulted the snake into the air, end over end it flew like a boomerang, but fortunately this boomerang was on a one-way route. Seconds passed with silence. Jack and Edgar looked up into the sky and noticed the snake plummeting from the puffy clouds until... *splash!* The snake hit the water. It paused and probably thought *What the heck was that all about?* It lay still for a few more seconds until it feverishly swam away in the other direction, unharmed.

Edgar and Jack stood and dusted themselves off from their terrifying ordeal. Catching their breath, the two reflected on the strange sequence of events. Jack turned to Edgar and asked, "What's my back look like?"

"L-Looks like a b-big b-bite!" Edgar said, trying to pad Jack's tough ego, even though the mark was no bigger than an average pimple.

"Aww, man, I bet! That thing had fangs. It even had a rattler, I think. I heard it!"

"But you're all right, man," Gene said. "But let me put a Band-Aid on that bite."

"Probably need one the size of a bed pillow," Jack said.

More like a postage stamp, Gene thought.

Gene stood and brushed off, before making a straight line to his bag, grabbed his canteen, and drew a long swig. Then he dumped some water on Jack's back.

Edgar removed the small first-aid kit from Gene's backpack. Jack laughed. "You're such a boy scout."

"Always prepared. But I'm not sure about you, Mr. Didn't-Bring-a-Canoe," Gene jabbed.

Gene opened an alcohol swipe and rubbed it over the tiny mark left by the snake. It hadn't broken the skin. He placed a Band-Aid over the area. "There, you'll be fine."

"Yeah, we better get going before anything else happens," Jack said.

The three grabbed their bags and hiked off down the trail.

Jack pulled out the map. "All right, guys. We have maybe two more miles and we're there, I think."

"Hallelujah!" Gene said, before he and Edgar high-fived.

The terrain transitioned from hard-packed dirt to a much more rugged, jagged-rocky trail. They noticed that the creek and trail descended rapidly, and the water became more turbulent. But with that came breathtaking views of the rapids and the pines that shaded the banks.

"Look, guys. It's a bald eagle. On that tree." Gene pointed.

The three stopped and gazed at the eagle perched on an overhanging tree.

"Are you sure, Gene? Its head's not bald," Jack said.

"No, Jack, it's a bald eagle. Their heads aren't 'bald.' They're white and don't change until they get older. I learned all about them at summer camp last year," Gene said.

The three marveled as the bird took flight. The Bandits watched until the majestic bird was out of sight.

Shortly after, Jack looked down the path and spotted a person about two hundred yards away.

"Oh, wow! We're not alone. Gene, quick, put the map in my backpack," Jack demanded.

As the man approached, they noticed how well dressed he was for the woods.

"Wow, he looks like he's going to an important meeting or something," Jack said.

The man had short, dark, gelled hair and a gold watch that glistened in the sun like a flashlight, a suit and brand new, very fancy shoes that could blind a man without sunglasses. He presented an air of importance.

"Hey, guys. How are you kiddos doin'?" the man said, with a hint of a Brooklyn accent.

"Oh, we're doing good. Just out for a little hike, you know?" Jack answered. He swallowed and stepped back. Something about this man made him uncomfortable.

"It's really beautiful in these parts. I just try to take in every second of it," the man said.

"Oh, we know. We come here all the time," Jack said.

"Well, have a good hike." The man smiled, exposing not-so-white teeth. Jack didn't think the man's teeth went with his clothes. But he shrugged it off.

The Bandits walked down the path, turning their backs to him, but they could still feel the man watching them.

"Hey, guys!" the man called.

Jack turned. "Um, yeah, what's up?"

"You aren't a Mathias, are ya?" the man asked, squinting.

"Yeah, how'd you know?" Jack asked.

"Oh, my heavens, I used to work with your dad. Your dad and I go way back. Is he still the VP of Sales at Solutions Systems?"

"I know he works there; don't know what he does, though," Jack laughed.

"I haven't seen him for a while; I really should call him. Actually, yeah, why isn't John out here with ya?"

Jack let out a nervous laugh. "Umm, I don't know. Um, I think he has some meeting or something today."

"Oh, right, I'm going to call him soon. I'll let him know I saw you on the trail."

Jack looked at Edgar and Gene. He waved his hands. "No. No. You can't call him. No, don't do that."

The man walked closer to the three. "Why? You guys aren't running away from home, are ya?"

"Um…" Jack said, flustered, once again looking at the Bandits, equally tongue-tied. "No."

138

The man burst into laughter before patting Jack on the back. "It's all good, just going for a little walk. I got ya. Hey, well, I'm Dan, nice to meet ya…" The man held out his hand for a handshake.

"I'm Jack. Nice to meet you."

"Hi, I'm Gene," Gene said, holding out his hand.

"Nice to meet ya," Dan said, shaking Gene's hand.

"E-E-Edgar," Edgar said with his voice quivering.

"Hi, Edgar," Dan said. "Well, hey, kiddos, if you have time, do you want to see something really cool here?" Dan asked.

"Sure," Jack said.

"There's a cave that has cool air that comes out of it, and it honestly feels like you're stepping into a refrigerator."

As they talked, Edgar scanned the strangely familiar man. He noticed a thick scar on his right hand. A sharp, knife-like pain turned in Edgar's stomach; fear shot down his spine as a memory flashed through his mind. A memory of the man in the hallway of his house, punching his brother while he watched through the crack of his bedroom door. Yelling. The same scent of cologne, hair, and the scar—the scar.

"Edgar? Edgar? You here?" Jack's voice echoed. "Come on, man. This guy's going to show us this cave that is like right up here. And it's awesome because cool air comes out of it. It's like nature's refrigerator, man."

"O-O-Okay," Edgar said, with a twinge of reluctance in his voice.

139

The four walked down the rock path before cutting off the trail and walking through some thick brush. As they walked through the brush, jaggers ripped through their skin.

"Ow, jeez. This better be worth it." Gene grimaced.

Finally breaking through the jaggers, they entered a clearing where a steep, downhill path transitioned and leveled out to an opening in the rock wall.

"This is it, kids," Dan said.

The boys stared at the opening.

"Oh, man. What are we waiting for? Let's go." Jack shrugged off his backpack. "Oh, crap, Gene, you didn't zipper the bag."

The map, letter, and Jack's underwear fell to the ground. Jack snatched the letter and map and held them to his chest.

"Whoa, what's that you got there?" Dan asked.

"Nothing, just—um—just a love letter," Jack said.

"Love letter?" the man said. "Kids don't do love letters anymore." He chuckled. "You guys' text that stuff. Besides, that paper looks really old. Like antique old."

"It's nothing really. Let's just check this cave out." Jack stepped toward the hole.

"Okay, okay." Dan bent down, inches from Jack's face "We will, but Daddy wouldn't be happy if he knew you were here, would he?"

"No, he can't know, actually," Jack said.

"So, I don't have to call Daddy, do I? So, tell me, what is it?" Dan's eyes grew wide.

Jack glanced over to Edgar and Gene, who were frozen like wet towels in a freezer. "All right, it's a map to a treasure," Jack said. "We found it buried underground in a chest."

"In a chest?" Dan laughed. "Let me see…"

Jack gave the man the letter and the map before turning to Gene and Edgar, with a listless look in his eyes. Dan smiled as he scanned the map and letter. The smile turned into contemplation. While it appeared, the wheels were turning in his head, the man handed the map and letter back to Jack.

"Kids…" Dan laughed and shook his head. "What I would do to be a kid again. You kiddos get excited about the silliest stuff, but it's fun. I wish I could go back and be a kid again!"

"Wait, so you think this is fake?" Jack blurted out.

"I'd hate to tell ya, kid, but it's as fake as Santa. But whatever gets you excited." Dan looked toward the cave. "Now, this here, this is real. There's no treasure, but you can see it, and it's right in front of your eyes. Unlike that fake thing in your hands." Dan laughed. "So come on. Let's check it out."

"I'm ready," Jack said.

"Me, too," Gene said.

Edgar didn't say anything.

"All right," Dan said. "Leave your bags here. I'll hand them to you then. Now, Jack, you and I will go in last, to help the others crawl into the cave."

"Okay," Jack said.

Gene headed into the cave first, soon followed by Edgar. Edgar shook his head and mouthed "NO" to Gene.

"Wait, what do you mean, Edgar?" Gene whispered.

"B-B-B-Bad m-man—he attacked m-m-my br-br-brother."

Jack went in next. "Whoah. It does feel colder."

"I know. Go farther in, it gets even colder," Dan said, throwing their bags into the cave. "You can explore for a bit. I have to get something quick."

Jack took a couple of steps farther into the dimly lit cave. "Come on, guys." His voice reverberated through the cavern.

"Jack, no, wait," Gene whispered. "I think this guy may not be good. Edgar knows him."

"He's fine, guys. He works with my dad. Everyone there dresses really nice. You can trust him, trust me."

"Wait. What's that sound?" Gene asked.

The three stopped and listened to what sounded like a rumbling train in the distance.

Jack put his ear to the cave wall. "Yeah, what is that?" he asked.

The noise echoed through the cavern walls, getting louder and closer, until... *Boom.* The light at the entrance of the cave went dark. The Bandits could barely see inches in front of their faces. Blindly, they crawled to where the opening once was and found a boulder covering the whole entrance.

"What's going on? Hello?" Jack screamed through the boulder.

"Help!" the three yelled, and they pounded on the wall for what felt like an eternity.

After no response, they stopped and put their ears to the boulder, listening for any noise outside.

But all they could hear was the sound of someone running away.

Chapter 19
Grocery Store Run-In

At the local Boonetown Mr. Z's Grocery Store, Gene's mom, Cathy, pushed her squeaky cart down the bread aisle. She had just pulled a loaf of Gene's favorite bread from the shelf when she spotted Jack's mom, Victoria.

"Hey, Victoria," she called with a wave.

"Hey," Jack's mom said. "How are you?"

"I'm good. Just stocking up while Gene's away on the crabbing trip."

"Me, too," Jack's mom said.

"You know boys; they'll eat you out of house and home. So how are you? Got summer plans?" Gene's mom asked.

Jack's mom shook her head. "Well, we wanted to, but Jack has summer school. So, we may do a quick vacation in August, but we're not sure. How about you?"

"Well, we're not sure either. I didn't tell Gene yet, but I got an out-of-state job offer, and I'm probably going to take it, since I am the breadwinner and all…" Gene's mom held the bread up in the air.

"Oh, wow. Congratulations. Good for you." The two exchanged hugs. "But that will be tough on Jack and

Gene, though. They've spent so much time together over the years."

"I know." Gene's mom nodded. "But this is such a good opportunity. I can't turn it down."

"No, no, of course not." Jack's mom pulled a bag of Krispy K Chips from the shelf and tossed it into her nearly overflowing cart.

Gene's mom followed suit and dropped two bags of chips into her cart, which was not nearly as full.

"But at least they're getting to spend time together now." Jack's mom pushed her cart down the aisle. "Actually, speaking of that, did you hear anything from them at all?"

"I haven't actually, but they're probably having a blast, so I haven't been too concerned. Well, okay, maybe a little. But he often goes over to Edgar's. His dad's nice."

"Yeah, he always seemed nice at the PTO meetings years ago. But you know how us moms are always worried about our boys…" Jack's mom said with a smile.

They pushed their squeaky carts up the aisle toward the checkout line. As they walked and talked, Gene's mom noticed Edgar's dad walking out of the store with groceries. "That's Edgar's dad. How can he be here if they're in Maryland?" Gene's mom yelled. She hurried outside and tried to catch him.

"Come back… Come back!" she yelled as he pulled out of the parking lot, oblivious to the commotion.

Jack's mom ran outside, and they looked at each other.

"What do you think is going on?" Gene's mom asked.

"I don't know, but I smell a rat and his name is Jack. I'm sure they're up to something," Jack's mom said as she pulled her phone from her handbag. "I might have the father's number. I'll call and see what's what."

"Good idea. My phones in the car," Gene's mom said.

Jack's mom flicked through her phone contacts and found the number. "Gee, I haven't spoken to him in a long time. My husband talked to him when he called the other day. I don't think I've talked to him since the divorce." She tapped on the number.

"Hello, this is Frank."

"Frank, it's Victoria, Jack's mom."

"Oh, wow, a voice from the past. How are you?"

Jack's mom quickly rattled off the story and learned that Edgar's dad had nothing to do with the weekend.

"Okay, thank you. I'll handle it."

She clicked off the phone. "The boys are not with Edgar's father."

Cathy grabbed Victoria's arm. "Oh no! Then—then where are they?"

"I'm calling 911!" Jack's mom yelled.

146

Chapter 20
Bandits Get the Big-Mo

The trapped Boonetown Bandits punched, pushed, and kicked the boulder that blocked their escape from the cave. Every vein popped out of their necks, arms, legs, and foreheads. Edgar was the first casualty and fell to his knees, gasping for air. Gene shortly followed him. Jack exerted every inch of himself, but to no avail. He fell to his knees and huddled beside Edgar and Gene.

"What the heck are we going to do? I can't believe this. How could a guy who knows my dad do this?" Jack asked.

"H-He d-didn't," Edgar said.

"What do you mean?" Jack and Gene asked.

"L-Look at y-your bag," Edgar said.

Jack opened his pack and pulled out a lighter. Jack flicked it a few times to get it lit before putting it an inch or so away from the pack.

"Solutions Systems, John Mathias, VP of Sales," Jack read.

"You're right, Edgar," Gene said.

"He just read my bag." Jack threw his lighter into his pack. "He didn't know my dad. He's a con, a big

147

smooth-talking con artist." Jack balled his hands into fists.

"H-He attacked my br-brother," Edgar said.

"Ugh, seriously?" Jack asked, dejected. "Edgar, you have to tell us this kind of stuff, especially if you know something we don't. That's teamwork. That's how you find the solution."

"Wow, Jack. Are you all right? You mean Jack can't do it all?" Gene asked.

"Yeah, well, I am pretty awesome, but working together is the only thing that'll get us out of this cave."

"Well, we have to figure something out. Let's brainstorm here. What do we need most right now?" Gene asked.

"L-L-Light," Edgar said.

"Yes, exactly," Gene agreed. "Let's look around with your lighter, Jack. If we can find something to burn, we can see; and if we can see, we can figure out what we have to work with to get out of here."

"Wow," Jack said. "That's the first step! If we can see, we can at least work toward getting out of here."

"Umm, yeah, that's pretty much what I just said," Gene joked.

The Bandits scoured through their bags for anything flammable.

"Okay, so…" Gene looked the things over with the lighter in hand. "We have a pair of underwear, two pairs of socks, and hmmm… body spray." Gene looked at Jack. "Body spray?"

"Hey, you never know, Gene, who you're gonna run into."

"Yeah, whatever makes you feel better, Jack. But seriously, grab the underwear and socks, then roll them all together and twist them until they're tight, like a wet towel. You know, like in gym class when you try to smack me."

Jack suppressed a laugh and followed Gene's instruction with ease.

"All right, now, Edgar," Gene said. "Now I want you to keep the lighter lit as much as possible."

"All right, here goes nothing," Gene yelled. He sprayed the body spray and *Pfffhshsh.* An explosion of flame shot like a flamethrower through the contours of the cave, reminiscent of a fire-breathing dragon.

"Agh!" Jack screamed, as the hair on his arms and fingers flamed up and disintegrated into thin air. The burning underwear dropped from his hand.

"Whoa! That was awesome…" Gene looked on in amazement, and Edgar chuckled.

Jack rubbed the dead skin follicles off his arms and stomped out the burning underwear. "You didn't do it right. Give it here, Gene. It's my turn."

"Wait. Hold up, Jack. Back up. We might be able to do it without your dirty underwear. Let me try with just the lighter and the body spray this time."

Gene sprayed the lighter and a hot, scorching, face-melting fireball shot out just as far as the first one. The bright flame added a little more context to the cave, which they thought resembled the inside of a giant's throat.

The cave's ceiling was three times their height, and about two arm's length in width, before it narrowed and descended rapidly farther underground. The walls were rigid, and stalactites shaped like icicles hung from the ceiling. The cave was cool to the touch and had a damp, earthy smell.

"Whoa. Give it here," Jack said. "I want to try. Man, if we get out of here, we can do this at home." Jack snagged the can from Gene and shot fireballs for his own entertainment. He went through three-quarters of the can's contents with a continuous light show.

"All right, stop, Jack," Gene snapped. "You're wasting the spray."

Jack and Edgar looked toward Gene.

"Hand me the lighter. There's nothing here, except rocks and old pieces of wood. We'll have to go deeper into the cave."

Gene took the body spray from Jack and shook it. "Really? Our lives are on the line, and you used almost all of it? I don't even know if we can make it now."

Dejected and frustrated, the Bandits made their way deeper into the cave, one quick spray at a time. Gradually they transitioned from the vestibule section to the deeper, narrower part of the cave, as the body spray was about to hit empty. Jack took a step in the dark and...

Slump. Jack's feet ripped through the loose dirt floor, and he fell several feet below. Jack's body thumped to the ground.

"Jack, are you okay?" Gene yelled down into the darkness.

Groans. Jack slowly moved and wiped the dirt off his clothes.

"Yeah, I'm okay, I think. Actually..." Jack felt a pillow-like bag below him.

"Guys, throw me the hairspray. I feel like I landed on a bag or something"

Gene and Edgar stared down the dark hole, while Gene tossed the hairspray, which thumped on the ground in front of Jack.

Jack lit the lighter with his left hand and bent down, inspecting what he landed on.

"Hmm, it's..." Jack brushed off the dust, "It's a big bag, and it looks like there are letters on it."

Gene and Edgar waited patiently.

"Well, what do those letters say, Jack?" Gene nudged.

"Hold on, hold on." Jack bent down closer. "It says, important—oh, wait, no! Imported Sugar. It's a big bag of sugar," Jack said, surprised, before standing up and using the hairspray to light up more of the area.

"Oh, wow, there's like tons of bags of sugar down here."

The Bandits all were perplexed at why there would be bags of sugar in an underground cave.

"W-W-Wait! A-Actually my br-brother has big b-b-bags of sh-sugar at our h-house, too," Edgar said.

"Interesting, Edgar," Gene said, "and it's weird because that guy's been at your house, you said."

Jack turned to the small area behind him and illuminated the wall with the lighter and hairspray.

"Oh, shoot, there's something carved in the wall," Jack yelled as he got inches away from the wall and lit the lighter.

"It says, I MISS U—" Jack read left to right before he moved the lighter down the wall and read, "Papi and Johnny—" Jack relit the lighter and went toward the floor and continued, "Did i—" Jack combed the wall with the lighter, looking for more words. "It looks like they started another letter beside the 'I,' but I don't see anything else here."

"Wait, Jack, is there a comma or period anywhere in there?" Gene asked.

"Dude, I don't see one. Who puts a comma or period when they're carving into a rock?"

"Yeah, true," Gene agreed. "But a comma would clarify some things, like if they miss Papi and Johnny, or if they're trying to say they miss their loved ones and telling whoever finds this that Papi and Johnny did something."

"W-Wait" Edgar interrupted. "J-J-Johnny is the real n-name of the g-guy who st-stuck us here. And P-P-Papi is his b-boss. Th-Those t-two and another g-guy, Br-Bruno, beat my br-brother up."

Silence filled the cave as the severity of the predicament set in. The Bandits were in way over their heads.

Knowing that the mood needed to be shifted, Jack pressed on.

"Okay, well, they're not here, so we just have to get out of this cave. Let me just check if there's anything else before you guys help me up out of here."

Jack bent down and flicked the lighter toward the wall and saw something between the bags of sugar and dirt floor underneath. He reached down and grabbed it.

"It's a wallet," Jack yelled up before he opened it and thumbed through it. "No money, dang! But there's a driver's license." Jack pulled it out and brought it to his face. "Mike Evans, five foot nine with brown eyes and glasses. And he's an organ donor, that's nice!"

"M-Mike Evans?" Edgar mumbled through quivered lips.

"Mike Evans?" Gene said with a crack in his voice. "That's the guy who's been missing for a few months."

"Th-That was my br-brother's fr-friend," Edgar said.

"Oh, wow, well, he was here," Jack yelled up before bending down and scouring around more.

Gene and Edgar waited and looked down at Jack, only being able to make out flickers of light from Jack's lighter.

"Oh, hey, there's something else," Jack called up.

With the lighter in his left hand, he picked up the corner of the bag closest to the wall. When he looked closer, he saw something. Fear shot down his spine like a lightning bolt. His breath stopped, and his heart torpedoed like a skydiver falling without a parachute.

Inches away from the lighter, he saw the same glasses from the driver's license picture. But these had bent frames and cracked lenses. And the lenses were covered with what he hoped was just mud. Jack let go of the bag and dry-heaved.

"Jack, what is it"?" Gene asked.

Jack took short, deep breaths to compose himself. "Give me a minute."

"Y-Y-You okay, Jack?" Edgar asked.

Jack, knowing the hysteria it would cause, fought his impulses to freak out, and chose to block out what he may have seen for the sake of the Bandits.

What good would that do? It could've been anything. Right? Jack thought.

Jack stood up, looking up in the direction of Gene and Edgar. "All right, guys, let's get outta here. Here's the lighter." Jack threw the lighter up between Gene and Edgar. "Get that board we saw and lower it down and pull me up."

Edgar fetched and lowered the board down slowly. Jack felt for the board before hugging and latching on to it.

"Pull," Jack called up.

Gene and Edgar set their feet and pulled the board, and with only a few grunts, Jack was on solid ground in front of them.

Jack jumped to his feet and headed toward the entrance of the cave. "All right, let's do this!"

Gene glanced at Jack as he passed. "Are you okay, man? What did you see?"

"Nothing."

"Hmm, weird," Gene whispered to Edgar as they followed him.

Jack seemed possessed. He walked briskly through the dark like he was wearing night-vision goggles.

"Can you even see?" Gene called out to Jack.

"Yeah, I can." *Bang.* His shin greeted rock. "Ahhh... Fff..." Jack clenched his shin. Edgar leaned toward the sound of Jack's moaning and flicked the lighter to illuminate Jack. He then scanned the object that caused it—a rock.

"F-F-Fulcrum," Edgar said, looking up for assurance from Gene.

"Oh, yeah, like we learned in class. But..." Gene touched his chin and his eyes drifted up.

"I got it. The piece of wood! We'll use the board back there to make a lever. Wow, Edgar! Good thinking! Go grab it quick."

Jack stood gingerly and took the rear. Gene led the way with a lighter in hand, and Edgar, right behind, held the rectangular rock and the wooden board as they walked toward the entrance.

Edgar set the rock and board down by the blocked entrance. The sound of heavy rain smattered the boulder and thunder rolled outside. Small streams of water flowed through the cracks and into the cave.

"Oh, no…" Jack said. "It's really pouring."

"I bet the river is even faster now," Gene said. "Those rapids will be impossible."

"That's the least of our worries," Jack said. "Let's just get out of here first."

Jack glanced at Gene. He felt a little proud of what he just said. For the first time, his mind wasn't focused on getting the treasure and all the things he could purchase. He was truly concerned about his friends and getting out to safety. But, of course, he couldn't leave it at that. "Yeah, Gene, then it's on to that treasure."

Gene jammed the tapered side of the board in between the bottom of the boulder and the ground, while raising the top of it over his head. Edgar and Jack placed the rock on the ground under the board. Gene pulled down the board to create the lever. Grunting, Gene hoisted himself onto the board and anticipated the rock moving and a quick fall to the ground. He waited, and waited, and waited, still hanging.

"It's like playing seesaw with a sumo wrestler," Gene said. "I need more weight. Edgar, jump on."

Edgar moved toward Gene and grabbed him before lunging on top of him. Gene, who was now smashed between Edgar and the board, groaned. With the extra weight, Gene and Edgar fell to the cave floor, while the boulder lifted into the air and revealed the light from outside.

"Jack!" Gene yelled. "Grab the backpacks and get out!" He could hardly breathe since he was flattened under Edgar.

Jack grabbed the bags and jumped through the opening.

"Okay, Edgar. I don't weigh enough to hold the boulder up, so I'll go out next and Jack and I'll push the rock to the side when I get out," Gene said.

"Oh—okay," Edgar said.

Sliding between Edgar and the board, Gene broke free and noticed the weight of the rock had balanced out. Edgar floated higher and higher, almost to the tipping point. Gene's eyes glanced at the opening as it started to close.

Jack yelled through his hands like a megaphone. "Jump through! Jump through!"

Gene's world stopped. For the first time in his life, Gene felt like an athlete at the top of his game. He was in the zone; his eyes locked on the prize.

"I got this," Gene screamed ferociously, while he pounded his chest. He took off like a sprinter out of a starting block, and dove headfirst right through the opening, like a champion, hands in front of him, landing untouched. Well, the top half of his body…

"Agh!" Gene let out a bloodcurdling scream, his glasses and face caked in mud, teeth speckled with brown, gritty soil exposed, and his…

"Oh, man, Gene!" Jack cried. "Your legs are pinned. Oh, my god. This happened to some guy in Australia, and he had to cut off his own leg. You may have to do both," Jack yelled.

"Get it off me, Jack. Get it off me!" Gene screamed.

Jack groaned. He wrestled with the boulder, before losing his footing and falling face-first. He scrambled to his feet and continued, with heels locked into the mud, giving it his all, shouting, "You're not gonna take my best friends, you stupid boulder! You hear me? You hear me?" Jack gave the boulder one last shove. Miraculously, it worked! He managed to roll it off Gene. The opening was free! The Bandits were free! They'd escaped!

But.

Whack.

The wood under the boulder whacked Jack between the legs while Edgar fell to the cave floor.

"Agh!" Jack catapulted into the air, kicking and screaming, before making his return trip, still kicking and screaming. "Agh!" *Wham.* Mud flew when he made a face-first landing beside his best buddy, Gene.

Edgar crawled through the hole. He sat beside his friends while they groaned in pain.

"Oh, man," Jack said after a few moments. "This trip is wearing on me a bit." He looked at Gene. "Are you all right? Are your legs broken?"

Gene lifted his body off the ground. "Not broken, but I sure do hurt." He limped a little.

Edgar and Jack grabbed the soaked bags, while Gene looked around and pondered their next move. With rain rushing down Gene's forehead, he said, "Guys, what should we do? We don't have a map, and the river will be too high. Should we just go back?"

Jack paced. *No map, we're soaked, the river's too high, problem, problem, problem.* He walked up to the top of the trail and scanned the river up and down, his eyes locking in on the...

"The tree. Guys, come here." Jack pointed enthusiastically. "The birch tree the bald eagle was on. Let's walk across it, make it to the other side, and run back to Lito's."

Gene's and Edgar's faces did not show the same excitement as Jack's, but they agreed.

"All right, Jack," Gene said. "I'm not thrilled about the tree but getting back to Lito's probably is our best option."

The three hurried up the trail that was slowly turning into a small tributary. Jack approached the white-and-black-etched birch extending over the water. He gazed down at the rushing, rising whitewater below. With walls of rain falling on him, Jack projected his voice to Gene over the roar of the river. "This is no Spangler's, man. This is the real deal. If you fall, grab on to the tree." Gene nodded. Edgar cringed.

Jack jumped onto the tree. He felt a little give and wobbled to catch himself. While taking a deep breath, Lito's voice filled his head: *"Believe, find the solution, take one step until you reach the destination."* His shoes slipped a bit off the slippery birch. He swayed to the left, bent his knees, put his arms out, adjusted, took a step, and another, and another, just like he did on the high wire. The loud noise became white noise as he thought about little Spangler's Creek. Nothing, nothing will throw him off until… His feet hit the safe ground on the other side. He made it. Gene and Edgar hooted from the other side.

"All right, Gene! You're next!" Jack yelled.

Gene took a deep breath and stood on the tree. He stepped one foot onto the limb and hollered, "Guys! I forgot my bag beside the cave. I have to go grab it!"

He hopped off the log and dashed back toward the cave.

"Well, all right, Edgar. It's your turn, then!" Jack yelled.

Edgar approached the limb. "I-I can't d-do this. I'm too h-heavy."

"It's the only way, Edgar. You have to believe. I believe in you, Edgar. We can do this," Jack encouraged.

"Are y-you sh-sh-sure?"

"Positive!" Jack called, even though he was also devising a plan to get Edgar out of the water if he fell. "Come on, Edgar, one step at a time. Believe…"

"I b-b-believe. I b-believe. I believe…" Edgar said, with more confidence each time. Edgar stepped onto the tree, and like a kid possessed, eyes focused, one step at a time, he went. The rain and water deflected off him. A smile blossomed on his face, while in his mind, he was on a boardwalk, a very flat boardwalk. He took it all in as he walked confidently to the very end. His feet touched the solid ground. Jack jumped on him in celebration while Gene yelled from the other side.

"Woo-hoo! Yeah, Edgar, you're the man!" Gene yelled.

"Y-Your turn, Gene!" Edgar hollered across the river. "It's easy-p-p-peasy!"

Jack smacked Edgar on the back. "That's right, man. Let's go!"

Gene took a deep breath. "Ready or not, here I come!" Gene set his foot on the limb. He was just about to take the next step when, *SPLASH*.

Chapter 21
Here's Johnny!

Startled, the three stared at the impossible. The tree, Gene's only hope to get across the river, floated downstream before getting ripped into shreds by the churning rapids. Their one ray of hope became driftwood in the blink of an eye.

"Ugh! Now what?" Gene yelled.

Jack and Edgar looked at each other. Edgar pointed upstream. "The sw-swimming hole—"

"That's right!" Jack called. "Go up to the swimming hole. We'll follow up this side. If you jump off the cliff and swim, you can probably make it across."

Gene's heart raced. *The current's too strong right now, even in the calmer section, but jumping off the cliff is probably the only chance I have.*

"Okay, I'll meet you up there. But wait—" Gene bent down and picked up a palm-sized rock and put it in his bag to add more weight.

"Here, catch, man!" Gene launched the bag, and Jack caught it on the lower end of the bank.

"Close one!" Jack yelled.

The Bandits, on opposite banks, meandered their way along the river. As Gene ascended up his side of the trail, solo, he kept an eye out for the man who trapped them in the cave. About three hundred yards ahead, he spotted the back of the cliff: *the swimming hole.* The rain began to subside while the river from other smaller tributaries continued to rise. He glanced at the cliff ahead and darted for it.

He approached and rounded the trail by the cliff but stopped when he heard muffled voices echo around the corner. He halted, rested the back of his head to the cliff, and listened.

"Hey, Papi, it's me, Johnny. See, here's what I did. I'm here with Bruno. I have the money, but we're a little sidetracked," the man who called himself Dan said, talking on the phone before covering up and whispering. "And that boulder spot, it's gonna have to be a grave for someone else. Looks like Bruno's gonna get to live another day, I guess." Dan uncovered the phone, and shouted to the man standing in the water, "Anyways... what ya think, Bruno? About four hundred miles, give or take, from the Poconos? That about right?" Dan asked Bruno.

Gene threw his hand over his mouth to keep from shouting. He contorted his body around the edge of the jagged rock wall and peaked around. His eyes tunneled in like binoculars on Dan, the man from the cave, who was talking on the phone. There was also a makeshift raft made from driftwood and barrels, floating in the stained water, with a man holding it. The man, Bruno, was much heavier and less put together, with an unshaven face, curly black hair, and several layers of shiny necklaces camped out inside a forest of chest hair.

"Yeah, it's about four hundred miles, give or take," Bruno said, with a deep voice and hand gestures. "Just tell Papi we'll meet him tomorrow night. We have to hide out in the woods overnight. Cops were looking for us and somethin' just came up. We got some things to find."

Gene's heart thundered in his chest. *Wow, Jack was right, this guy's a pro. A professional crook.* He took a deep breath to avoid passing out before he leaned against the front of the wet, cool rock wall. He pressed his face against the wall and peered around the corner. Water dripped from above and splashed onto the tiny notches, and sediment splashed under his glasses, directly into his eye.

"Agh!" Gene yelled—he couldn't help it. Something sharp dropped into his eye. Pain crippled him as he extracted the thing from his retina. With blurred vision, he stood, planted his feet on the ground, tightened his core, and started to run. He took three strides behind the cliff when...

"Freeze. Don't move," Dan's voice permeated the air.

Gene raised his hands. It was more an instinct than anything.

"Ya think you can escape from the cave, but you don't know who you're messin' with. I'm not Dan. I'm-a Johnny 'Soft Hands!' You may have heard-a me." He motioned for Gene to move toward him.

Gene walked until the barrel of the gun was just inches away from his face. Gene inspected it closely. *It looks exactly like on television, every inch of the gun, the barrel, handgrip, and the magazine. The gun looks cold as steel.* His mouth dried up as he swallowed. A bitter, steely taste filled his mouth. Gene's world stopped. He took a deep breath. The smell of fear filled his nose, along with a slight aroma of chocolate. *This guy must have just eaten chocolate.* Gene was a mess.

Johnny let out a cynical laugh, showing his teeth through a dangerous smirk. The man motioned toward Gene with the gun. Gene's mind raced. *Should I kick him? He has a gun. He'll kill me.* Johnny's finger wrapped around the trigger. Gene prayed and thought of his mom, but it was too late. All of his dreams soon would be ending at the hands of a cold-blooded killer. Now there would only be two Bandits. He closed his eyes and...

Bang.

Chapter 22
Back to Lito's

Johnny's face turned white, his mouth puckered inward, and his pupils hid in the top of his head. A snake had chomped and latched onto his inner thigh.

Splash. Gene watched as the gun dropped into the water, submerged, then floated downstream. Gene looked up at a long snake dangling inches from his face, coming from Johnny's thigh. The man squirmed and screamed, "Get it off-a me! Get it off!"

Gene didn't waste a second and took off running.

***

Edgar and Jack looked on from the other side.

"Quick. Come with me, Edgar." Jack jumped into action.

Running full speed into the woods, Jack's eyes scanned for just the right tree. He found it and pointed toward it.

"Edgar, bend over behind that tree, and put your weight on it. I'm gonna break it."

Jack backed up, got a good running start, and lunged into the air headfirst, and clotheslined the tree. The bottom half of the sapling peeled like a banana. Jack and Edgar jumped on the flexible tree like a trampoline until it fully detached. Jack picked it up and sprinted to the bank and pulled four pieces of rope from Gene's bag.

"All right, Edgar. This stick is our fly rod. We need to catch Gene with it. We have to tie these pieces of rope together so we can throw it out to Gene when he swims across." Jack and Edgar furiously knotted the ropes together.

***

Twenty feet up the cliff, Gene clenched tightly to the ledge with Bruno holding his foot. Bruno reached up and grabbed the back of Gene's neck.

"You know how many people I've killed just like you, huh?" Bruno asked.

Shaking, Gene had no answer. Bruno pulled out his knife from the sheath on his belt, raised it high, aiming for Gene's neck, and stopped.

"What's that sound?" Bruno turned. An object like a boomerang was headed straight for him.

"Snake!" Bruno screamed. Just seconds before, Johnny flung the snake, and it now wrapped itself around Bruno's neck. Bruno fell to the ground. Gene climbed to the top of the cliff. He spotted the Bandits, waiting for him in knee-deep water on the other side.

"Gene!" Jack yelled, as he practiced his fly-casting abilities. "Jump as far as you can. The minute you hit, start swimming, and grab the circle at the end of the rope!"

Gene swallowed deep and stepped to the edge. He trembled at the height and the rising water. He glanced back at the men having an epic battle with the water snake. He knew there was only one thing to do. Jump.

"Agh!" Gene flew, holding his glasses through the air, and "Agh!"

Splash. He plunged into the water. His feet hit the bottom of the river, body cold, his hands opened while his glasses drifted into the current. His calves flexed as he lunged off the bottom and surfaced. Gene, with his eyes blurry, spotted Jack, and made a straight line for the bank. Gene swam and looked up. His stomach rolled when he noticed the current had taken him farther back than where he started. The flow of the river was too fast. Gene looked back and was coming closer to shooting between the two cliffs into extreme whitewater.

Jack flung the rope back and forth like a professional angler. Flying through the air, the rope landed a few feet in front of Gene. He reached, but the current pulled him away.

Jack pulled the rope in and tried to recast.

"Jack—quick! Help!" Gene yelled in desperation. Exhausted, he turned around, and prepared to go between the rock walls through the spillway. Horrified, Jack made one last cast toward Gene. Jack, with laser beam focus, threw the rope. Flying through the air with perfection, the rope, with a nice tight cast, sailed ever so perfectly.

168

Gene prayed. "I love you, Mom, Dad. Please, someone, save me. Please!"

And like a halo from the heavens—or a lasso around a steer—the rope landed with precision over Gene's head and around his neck.

"Ugh-ugh," Gene choked out, startled and gasping for air he clenched the rope in tight fists.

Jack yelled, "Grab ahold of it, you idiot! We're going to pull you in!"

Gene managed to get the rope from around his neck. He held on to it for dear life.

Jack, in waist-deep water, pulled back on the rod. The sapling rod bent and bowed. Jack wondered how much more it would bend until it broke, along with his observation of Edgar's questionable knot-tying capabilities. Jack was pulled past the eddy line into the current.

"Edgar, grab my waist!" Jack yelled.

Edgar grabbed Jack, held him like a rag doll, and became a pillar of strength. Sure-footed, Jack brought the rod down and pulled the rope as Gene appeared larger in the horizon. Like pulling in a big flathead or blue catfish, Jack's arms tensed, his face grimaced, and his torso engaged in pulling in his best friend.

Jack and Edgar sighed when they saw Gene's face and heard his voice coming back, safe and sound.

"Oh, man," Jack said. "I thought we lost you for sure."

Gene floated on his back. His chest was falling and rising with each labored breath. "Thanks, man. Me, too."

Jack bent at the waist and panted. "We need you, Gene. You're one of the Bandits."

Edgar extended his hand to Gene and helped him get to his feet. "Thanks, Edgar."

"Glad y-you d-didn't drown."

The Bandits caught their breath along the bank of the roaring river before they grabbed their bags. Gene pulled out his extra pair of glasses, and the three ran off into the dusk toward Lito's.

"You're gonna pay for this, ya hear? You're gonna pay," Johnny and Bruno yelled across the water as the boys disappeared.

Jack turned in time to see Johnny raise the map. "And we still got your map!"

***

"Freakin' snake, that freakin' thing! If I wasn't so afraid of it, I woulda killed it," Johnny said.

"I know what ya mean. Those things scare me," Bruno agreed.

"Hey, Bruno, I say we-ah wait till the mornin' to get this here treasure. Call it a day, huh? What do ya think?"

"Sounds like a plan. Hey, did ya notice that portly kid? I think he's that brother. He's always in his room, eating chips and salsa," Bruno laughed.

"Ya know, I think you're right, Bruno. Well, as soon as we get this here treasure…" Johnny smiled as he looked at the map. "We're gonna make a stop and make all of 'em pay, and that little Jackie boy and his dorky friend. I mean, who do they think they are? And don't kids watch crime shows anymore? I don't think they even know who we are. Well, they'll regret messin' with America's Most Wanted Criminals, huh?"

***

Even though they were exhausted, the Bandits kept running toward Lito's. The sky was darkening, and Edgar wanted to stop and rest, but Jack hurried him along. Edgar nearly fell over, but when Jack pointed out what looked like a tall monster, they screamed and kept running.

"No! It's a bear!" Jack yelled.

Edgar looked back as his feet hit a root. "Agh!" Edgar fell; his heart pounded faster. He stumbled back to his feet.

"Come on. Come on…" Jack waved his hands toward him. "He's gaining on us!"

The Bandits hustled down the trail. Gene looked back and noticed the eyes were awfully low to the trail and moving like it was jumping. Rather than stopping to find out what it was, they rounded the corner and ran another two hundred yards as the eyes disappeared behind them. Their sprint slowed to a jog, and Gene, slightly out of breath, said, "Jack—" as he hunched over, breathing deeply. "I'm pretty sure that's not a bear. It's too low to the ground. It looked like it was hopping."

Jack stopped, not nearly as winded, and answered, "No, bears get low when they're stalking people. Trust me, it's a bear, or there's a slight chance it's a chupacabra, but I'd bet on a bear."

The three continued, jogging for another quarter mile, exhausted, until they smelled something in the air. *Sniff sniff.* Jack stopped. "You smell that?" Jack asked. "Smells like... hickory. Oh, wow. We're almost there. It's coming from Lito's yurt."

The Bandits bumped fists and found their second wind and raced to Lito's camp.

Jack arrived first, followed by Gene, and then Edgar came in a few minutes behind. Lito walked out of his yurt with a bowl of something in his hand.

"Hey, Lito. Oh, my god, we're so glad we found you!" Jack gasped.

"Well, hey, there, Jack. Good to see ya, buddy. Y'all decided you loved the woods so much, you're gonna stay here another night, I'm guessin'?"

Gene stepped in. "No, Lito, we have a lot to tell you."

"It was crazy," Gene blurted.

"A snake bit me," Jack yelled.

"It flew through the air," Gene said.

"We had a map," Jack called.

"J-Jack th-thought he was n-nice," Edgar added.

"I saved the day," Jack exclaimed.

"I had a gun in my face," Gene hollered, and he gave Jack a shot on the arm.

Lito's face turned red, and he outstretched his arms. "Boys, enough. Settle down. I can't follow your train of thoughts."

The Bandits stopped talking. They nodded, and Jack said, "I'm just glad we found you."

Lito continued, "Jeez, all right, all right. It was crazy, I get y'all. But no need to be all crazy about it again, talkin' a mile a minute. Where's that gonna get you? Nowhere! Now, if you want to find a solution, the first thing you gotta do is tell me, in a calm, orderly manner, what happened."

Jack and Gene exchanged looks. Jack said, "You tell him, Gene, you're better at explaining than me."

Gene smiled. "Thanks, man." He told Lito all about the treasure map and the snake and the cave and about Johnny "Soft Hands"; his voice wavered at that part. When he was finished with the story, he said, "And that's why we decided to find you. Thought you could help us."

Lito leaned back and let out a hearty laugh. "Of course, I'll help. Y'all can stay as long as you want. And those two guys are criminals. That's for darn certain." He pushed some embers in the campfire. "First thing tomorrow we can take my canoe out. And we'll be off. Unless y'all wanna use your canoe?"

The Bandits looked at each other, then Gene said, "Umm, we don't really have a canoe, or kayak. Really, we don't have anything to make it down the river."

Lito looked at all three. "Wait, let me get this straight. Y'all wanted to find the treasure at Shotgun Falls, but you didn't have any raft? Well, how the heck did ya plan to do that?"

Jack laughed nervously. "Well, we just figured we'd make it happen. You know, find a solution."

Lito shook his head but cracked a smile. "Ya know, I love your spirit, Jack. I do. But sometimes being all piss and vinegar can get you in trouble. Finding a solution and overcompensating because you're unprepared and procrastinating is a recipe for disaster. Well, ya know, enough with the talkin'. Why don't you boys put those wet clothes by the fire, get a bowl of my rock bass jambalaya, and take a seat."

The boys sat around the small campfire and enjoyed their nice home away from home and contemplated things.

Gene said, "Actually, Lito, I think if I could, I'd love to stay and live like this. You have everything you want."

Edgar nodded. "M-Me too."

Lito filled their bowls with stew. "Eat up. You're gonna need your strength."

Jack chimed in. "Yeah, Lito. After I serve my grounding, you mind if I live with you a couple weeks, and then maybe when I get older…"

"Stop, boys," Lito said. "This ain't your dream. This was my dream. Do like I said: live your own life and experience things. And honestly, boys, I'm not even sure if this is my ideal life anymore either."

The Bandits locked eyes with each other and then looked back to Lito.

"What do you mean, Lito?" Jack asked.

"Things change. You meet people, and what ya want changes. And honestly, after meeting you guys, I got thinkin' about when I was a counselor at a camp. It was up the Appalachians. Making a difference and changing kids' lives just excites me. And running into y'all made me think."

Edgar stood up and walked toward Lito, hugged him, and said, "You ch-ch-changed me."

Gene and Jack looked at each other, surprised by Edgar's fondness for Lito.

Lito wiped a tear from his eyes. "Thanks, Edgar, I appreciate that, I really do. Anyway, who knows, I may just stay here till I die, but it's just a thought." Lito cleared his throat and shifted topic. "So how about we attack that river and find that gold tomorrow? Huh?" Lito clapped his hands.

"Sounds good. I'm excited," Jack said.

"Well, ya better be ready. I never even ran Shotgun Falls. Always been too scared," Lito said, laughing. "But always a first for everything."

Jack faced Lito and smiled, dismissing the severity of the situation. "Yeah, it'll be easy. I'm not even worried about it."

The Bandits and Lito got ready for bed, anticipating a wild, death-defying ride down the most challenging rapids most people have ever seen. As they prepared to lie down, Jack spotted the same eyes that chased them down the trail.

"Guys, look. It's back," Jack whispered.

"Oh, wow, is that what was chasing y'all?" Lito bit into his nightly apple.

"Yeah, I think. Why, what is it, Lito?" Gene asked.

Lito held in his laughter as he bit into his apple. "It's a vicious predator. It robs me all the time."

"What do you mean? Like it steals money or gold?" Jack asked.

"Just as important as that stuff: it stole eighteen carrots from me." Lito laughed again. "But I'm fine with it. Go on to bed, Jack," Lito said as he walked into the yurt.

Jack couldn't sleep right away. He paced and wondered: *is it eighteen karats of gold or diamonds? Why wouldn't he care? What does he mean?*

Gene, lying down and half asleep, opened his eyes and, since he could usually read Jack like a book, said, "It's a rabbit, Jack. He stole eighteen carrots. Good night."

"Ah, duh… Jeez." Jack rolled onto his side and closed his eyes, dreaming of gold.

Chapter 23
Shotgun Falls, Here We Come

"All right, boys. Rise and shine."

The boys awoke to the sound of sizzling, the smell of garlic and veggies in the air.

"Rise and shine, boys," Lito repeated. "Got breakfast cookin'."

Edgar and Gene were the first to wake up, that is, the first to get up and check out Lito's breakfast. Jack had not even stirred.

"What is it, Lito?" Gene asked.

"It's a veggie frittata. Got it from the garden. Now, I don't wanna lie, I do run into Mr. Zs to get eggs from time to time, but other than that, all natur-el." Lito laughed. "Let me go get you boys some plates."

"Well, look who's come back to the world..." Lito hitched his thumb toward Jack.

Jack wiggled like a caterpillar inside of his sleeping bag.

Lito placed four plates on the picnic table with napkins.

"So, are you boys excited for the rapids?" Lito asked.

"W-W-When it's over," Edgar said.

Jack stood up, yawned, and walked toward the table.

"I don't blame ya, Edgar," Lito said. "It's pretty rough. Three of the rapids are even bigger than the ones you see in movies." Lito grabbed the spatula and put the veggie frittata on Jack's plate.

Jack inspected it with his fork and eyes. "Wow, Lito, I'm impressed. I feel like I'm in the Hamptons. Not that I've ever been there. Just saw it on TV once and they were eating frittatas." Jack chewed his food.

The three shoveled food into their mouths, smiling and enjoying each bite.

"Lito, you should really be a chef," Jack said while Edgar and Gene nodded with their mouths full. "I'm serious. Everything you make is amazing. I don't even like vegetables, but I love this. It has a crunch to it."

"Shucks, thanks, boys. That means a lot. Yeah, I added a little protein today because I knew y'all would need a little extra strength to get through the rapids."

"What do you mean?" Gene asked. "What kind of protein?" Gene inspected his eggs a little more closely. "You mean these crunchy bits?"

"Those crunchy things have a lotta protein. Underneath the rotted wood over there"—Lito pointed toward the riverbank— "I hit nature's edible lottery. I found a bunch of grasshoppers and slugs for the frittata." Lito laughed and walked into his yurt.

"Yuck!" Jack's fallen fork rang as it hit the plate. Edgar spat frittata across the table, and Gene gagged while Lito laughed.

"Come on now," Lito said. "Just keep eatin'. You'll need all that energy."

Jack sucked in a deep breath. "I'm game." He swallowed every last bit.

Edgar managed to get it all down also, but Gene just ate around the crunchy bits. After the breakfast dishes were cleaned up, Lito assembled the boys. "All right. Today's a big day. You sure y'all wanna do this?"

They nodded. "You bet, Lito."

Lito clapped his hands. "All righty, then. I'll get our gear."

Edgar took a deep breath. "I'm sc-scared, guys."

Jack patted Edgar's back. "We all are, Edgar, but you want that treasure, right?"

Edgar nodded. "B-But what about J-Johnny?"

Gene coughed. "Yeah, man, he's a scary dude, but we got Lito on our side now."

"Sure," Jack said. "Nothing to worry about."

Lito walked out of the yurt with several paddles and life jackets.

The four made their way toward the river. As they approached, they looked out into the water and noticed it was still stained and running a little high.

They walked down the bank to the canoe. It was beautiful. Wood grains coursed the sides, with select woods ranging from reddish brown to light tan, and it had a nice glossy finish to it. And on the inside of the canoe, the well-crafted bracing made the vessel both strong and a work of art.

"Y'all like it?" Lito asked.

"Well, it's better than the one we have," Jack said, and they all laughed. "No seriously, man. It's gorgeous."

"I carved it myself. That's northern white cedar, very lightweight but strong wood. Then I stained it. I really like how the wood grains came out. This thing tracks like a dream, nice and straight." He looked at the Bandits and waggled his eyebrows. "Well, anyway, it can look as fancy as it wants, I guess, but the rapids will tip us regardless of how it looks." Lito laughed. "Anyway, real quick, 101 of canoeing. This is the stern." Lito pointed to the back of the canoe. "Most would say this is where the captain sits. The captain has to be strong and be able to guide and counter-steer."

Jack's hand shot up. "I'll be captain."

Gene gave him a shove. "Lito's the captain."

Lito didn't bother to correct Jack.

"Now, up here, this is the bow. It's the front of the boat." Lito tapped the bow. "Ya also want someone strong for power here." Lito winked at Edgar and patted him on the back. "The middle is where a good communicator comes into play. I'm looking at you, Gene." Lito smiled. "Other than that, for today we're just gonna call this the left and right side because the rapids don't care what we call them, and less thinkin' is less water drinking for ole Bessie here." Lito patted the canoe.

Jack whispered to Gene and Edgar. "Did he just say, 'less thinking is less water drinking'?"

"Did he just pat and call his canoe 'ole Bessie'?" Gene said, as Jack and Edgar smiled and shook their heads.

"Anyway, let's do this!" Jack yelled. "Or in the words of Gene, let's get this show rolling!"

The four set off from shore. Edgar sat in the front, Gene in the middle, and Jack and Lito in the rear. Once they were on the water, everything took on a new perspective. Jack couldn't help but admire the scenery. "It's so nice here."

"It sure is," Gene said."

"Nature at her best," Lito said. "Soak it all in, boys."

Edgar sucked in a deep breath and then smiled wide.

They were, for now, one with the river and embraced the wonderful feeling of being nestled between the evergreen-filled, lush mountain peaks. They spotted numerous wildlife; lots of colorful birds, ducks, and deer poked their heads out of rocks and pines along the Gauley. They paddled downstream and hit a few small ripples.

"All right, so there's a few things you gotta learn before it's too late," Lito said. "If I yell 'paddle right,' Edgar and Gene, you paddle on the right, and Jack and I will paddle on the left. Now if I say, 'draw right,' take your paddle out to the right of the canoe, and pull it in toward the canoe, which will pull the front right."

"Gotcha!" Gene called.

"Me, too," Edgar said.

"All right, we got it," Jack said. "So where are the rapids at?"

"They'll be here before you know it. These little riffles here are a good start, and we can practice here in the slow water, so we get closer to that ole unconscious competence," Lito said.

Gene looked at Jack before he asked. "It means to do something without thinking."

Jack shook his head and smiled. "Yeah, yeah, I knew that." Jack didn't know that.

Down the river they floated and practiced tightening up their skills, before relaxing. The canoe meandered around the corner, while Lito, Gene, and Edgar took in the peacefulness of the scenery. Jack decided to stand up to add more excitement.

"Sit down!" Lito hollered. "That's too dangerous."

But before Jack could sit on his own, a low-hanging branch helped him to his seat.

The sound of the rushing water was actually quite calming.

"I could fall asleep to this," Gene said. Then, just around the bend, they heard a much louder noise. As they looked off in the horizon line, the trees and water dropped.

"All right, Jack, you asked for it. We're comin' up on Rocky Falls," Lito said. "This is considered a class four, which is one of the smallest of the four we're doing today, but it's challengin'. Let's paddle over to the right side here and scout it out."

Under Lito's command, the canoe made a straight line to the bank. Edgar jumped out and pulled the canoe onto land while everyone jumped ashore. Lito took the lead as they walked to the side of the bank before the small cliffs to take a look. The four jumped on top of a boulder and scanned the river. The river dropped quite rapidly. The churning water created a wall of sound. Edgar and Gene glanced at each other, wide-eyed and open-mouthed, while Jack looked like a boy on Christmas morning.

"All right, boys. Here we are. Now, this rapid has about a thirty-foot drop, from the top of the rapid"—Lito pointed— "to the bottom, about three hundred yards downstream. That's pretty good, but y'all will wish you had this one later in the trip."

"Cool," Jack said. "Let's go!"

"Hold on," Lito said. "Now if ya look right there, in the middle..." He pointed to a place in the water. "See how that water ducks down and then goes up?"

"Oh, wow! It looks like one of the Flow Rider boogie board things they have at the water park," Jack said.

Lito laughed. "That's a hydraulic. That's when rushing water runs over a rock ledge or a boulder. I suspect there's a big boulder under there."

"L-Looks sc-scary," Edgar said.

Lito nodded. "It doesn't have to be scary if you know what to do. Now, luckily, I don't see any flatwater behind it, which means there may not be too much undertow, but it can be dangerous."

"Th-Thought so," Edgar said.

"It'll be all right," Jack said. "We're with a pro."

"Let's just say we want to try to avoid that," Lito said. "But the current is gonna try to push us into it. If it does, hold on and watch your drawers."

"Watch your drawers?" Gene asked.

"Pretty much means y'all may need a diaper," Lito said.

"Gotcha," Gene shot back with thumbs up.

"All right, so we go to the right of that, then we're gonna take a sharp right turn to avoid the rock wall. After that, we just go straight down the rapids until we find a calm spot on the bank to stop at."

Gene quickly asked, "What if we fall out?"

Lito shook his head. "Remember what I told ya? We're doomed if we talk about that now."

"Jeez, Gene. No one is falling out," Jack said.

"All right, let's not waste any more energy on that stuff," Lito said. "But all I'll say is, keep your feet up in front of your body, and kick for the shore. Now let's get floatin'."

The four pushed the canoe out into the water and paddled to the middle. They straightened out the canoe and headed on toward the rapid. Gene's and Edgar's hearts sank as the river disappeared in front of them.

Gene yelled back, "I feel like an old explorer, and we're going to fall off the side of the world!"

"Maybe you should feel like paddling, Gene, and we'll make it there a little faster!" Jack yelled.

As the start of the rapids came closer, Lito needed to holler over the raging water to get the Bandits' attention. "Now, we want to go in between those rocks!" Lito pointed. "You see how the water makes a V? It's called a downstream V. It means there's deeper water and no rocks. Now after we hit that V, paddle your butts off so we go to the right and not over that hydraulic."

Edgar let go a little scream.

"Me and Jack will compensate if need be," Lito continued. "Then we're making a sharp right, so we don't hit that rock wall. Really, boys, we just gotta go right, and after that, it should just take us down the middle of the rapids and we're home free."

They paddled the canoe and headed straight through the V. The front splashed, and Edgar's and Gene's dry clothes were drenched while Jack and Lito received a nice cool mist.

"Oh, yeah, woo-hoo!" Jack yelled as Gene's and Edgar's knuckles turned white from gripping the paddles. Their feet hooked around the floor bracing to keep them from bouncing out of the canoe.

"Paddle. Paddle harder!" Lito yelled.

The front of the canoe moved toward the right shore while the back of the canoe stuck out in the middle.

"Jack! Counter paddle, straighten it out. Straighten out!" Lito shouted even louder.

Jack paddled as hard as he could. The back end straightened out. He paddled with all his might. His arms ached, and sweat glistened on his face. Water splashed over the side, when he took one last stroke.

"Jack, no!" Lito yelled. "You straightened us out too far. The front's goin' toward the hydraulic. Edgar, Gene, quick! Paddle. Paddle harder!"

Gene and Edgar, bombarded by the chaos of the loud water, the speed of the current, and Lito yelling, looked ahead to see huge boulder tombstones approaching. Furiously they paddled to avoid a collision.

"Paddle harder, dig in!" Lito yelled.

The canoe headed straight for the hydraulic.

"Hold on. Hold on to your lunch," Lito yelled.

The front of the canoe dipped downward as Gene and Edgar screamed and were eye level with the water.

The front cut through, and water exploded onto Edgar and Gene. Suddenly the front shot up, and the sky was all they could see as they went up the hydraulic.

"Agh!" all four screamed.

The canoe, like a NASA rocket, shot into the air, flying high in the sky.

"Giddy up!" Lito yelled.

The canoe crashed back down into the water. The water splashed from the sides of the canoe. Jarred, all four fell to the floor of the canoe. Quickly, Lito, on his knees, grabbed the paddle. "Look out for that rock wall!"

Edgar groaned. The canoe practically bounced on the water.

"Quick, boys!" called Lito. "Quick, get up! Paddle. Paddle. Jack, counter paddle!"

They paddled with all their strength. The back of the canoe was inches away from crashing against the rock wall.

"Jack, counter paddle!" Lito called.

Jack, with his paddle out, swung the boat around parallel to the wall as they floated beside it.

"Phew…" The four let out a sigh of relief.

"That was close," Gene said, shaking his head.

"Yeah," Edgar said. "I th-thought we were g-goners."

"That was awesome," Jack hollered. "Let's get to the even bigger rapids." He stood and looked downstream at the next two hundred yards of smaller rapids in front of them.

"Jack. Sit down," Lito warned. "That was the hardest part, but we still ain't done with this rapid."

"Yeah, just checking it out," Jack said. "Man, this is a bit more than I thought. Everything's a bit faster and bigger when you're out here. But I'm sure we'll…" *BANG!*

Suddenly life got even faster. A shallow, small rock slammed the left side of the canoe. Jarred, Jack got knocked off kilter, and momentum took him over the side. His body thrashed through the violent up-churn. Water filled his nose, mouth, and airways, and his brain froze.

"Ahh!" Jack yelled. *Coughs*

A numbness overwhelmed him, and achy pains shot through his body. His jaw quivered and his body shook while being tossed and turned like a rag doll through the rapids.

"Feet up!" Lito yelled. "Swim downstream to shore, Jack!" Lito's words were muffled, at best, by the water and fear in Jack's racing mind.

"What?" Jack yelled through shivering lips.

The three looked on and paddled down the rapids.

Instinct and survival preservation settled in. Jack's feet rose in front, and his head lifted up as he kicked and paddled his arms downstream. He spotted a rock wall about twenty yards downriver. Floating fast, the wall approached rapidly. He swam, took one last lunge, and his fingers latched to the crevices on the slippery rock wall. He battled the current, pulling him downstream.

"Hold on. Hold on!" Lito yelled, well above the river.

Jack's grip weakened. He instinctively kicked his feet and lunged his stomach atop the rocky ledge. He crawled, stomach down, and his cold, cramping muscles gave all that was left to get his lower body out of the water.

He crashed on the rock, drenched, cold, and shaken. His teeth and body chattered. Jack's confidence wavered. He contemplated, *Maybe the people are right? This river is out of our league. Maybe this was just a crazy dream after all?* Like a fighter with lofty aspirations and a great prefight strategy, Jack got a first-round hook much harder than expected and it knocked him to the canvas, hard. And maybe staying down is a good thing. The easy thing, maybe? Round one: river wins with a knockout.

Or maybe not.

Suddenly Jack stood, strong and tall, because staying down wasn't in his blood. The treasure took a back seat. It was all about survival now. The river would have to earn round two. The Bandits won't go down without a fight.

Crashing through the rapids, Lito, Edgar, and Gene hung on for dear life. The canoe was filled with water but was just buoyant enough to find the bank downstream from Jack.

"Jack, buddy. You all right?" Lito asked.

"Yeah, I'm okay," Jack said, with teeth and body still chattering. "Just a scratch or two on my legs, but nothing major." He tried to downplay the situation.

"Ya look cold. But that's good, buddy. Yeah, if you're gonna fall out, that rapid, even though it's long, may be the safest one. So, you wanna walk the bank down to us?" Lito asked.

"Yeah, sure." Jack walked along the rocks toward the crew.

Lito, Gene, and Edgar grabbed the canoe at each end and dumped out most of the water before Lito stood it up on a rock to get any remaining water out. Gene and Edgar walked over to Jack sitting on the shore and gave him a pat on the back.

"All right, guys. Pretty good overall," Lito said. "It could have been a lot worse. Jack, good job paddlin', and great counter paddle by the rock, but make sure to have some touch when you paddle. You over-paddled and that's what got us in that predicament. Also, one step at a time, remember that?"

Jack nodded.

"It's universal. It's one paddle at a time, too. You did great navigating the big boulders, but you overlooked that small rock, and it came up and bit ya, didn't it?"

"Yeah, I guess," Jack said.

"You did good, though," Gene said. He patted Jack on the back.

"Boys, every rock can tip you the same way, so don't overlook the small ones. But also, Gene and Edgar, y'all are doing great," Lito added.

Jack stood, feeling a little angry. "Wait. I over paddled trying to fix their mistake. Why are you just getting on me?"

Lito shook his head. "Worry about yourself, Jack. I know what they need, and I know what you need. Pointing fingers ain't gonna get you in the captain's seat anytime soon, I can tell ya that."

Shortly after, they found their way to the canoe, but this time, it was filled with tension and not water.

"All right," Lito said. "Edgar, get in the front, Jack, you get in the middle, and, Gene, come on back to the stern with me." Lito and Jack exchanged glares.

They set off downstream and glided through the ripples of water, which paled in comparison to the last rapid. As the river flowed around the corner, the ripples dissipated, and the canoe entered into a wide pool area with cliffs on each side of the river.

"Oh, wait. This is the cliff area with the crazy snake and the robbers," Gene said.

Edgar pointed at the smoke in the woods while Jack sat quiet and stubborn as a bull, sulking at being benched for Gene.

"All right, boys. Let's paddle to shore quietly and check it out," Lito said.

Gene whispered and motioned. "Duck down low. If they see us, we're done."

The canoe approached the bank, and Edgar gently caught the bow before it hit the shore. They whispered to each other as Lito stood and assessed the scene. "From the looks of that fire, I'd say... Hmm, they probably left about a half hour or so ago."

"They're probably headed for the treasure," Gene said.

They walked along the bank as Lito checked for any signs.

"Bottles, plastic bags, paper plates, and trash bags. Well, they ain't foresters, I can tell you that. Look over there." Lito pointed toward the cliff. "They were draggin' something. Bet it's a raft, which means they're porting around this rapid. That'll help us make time. And they're in for a surprise because you can't port around the next rapids. After this one, you're in the lower gorge, and only helicopters and twenty-mile hikes through rocky rattlesnake country are getting you out."

"Oh, great. That's good to know, Lito," Gene said, while glaring at Jack.

As they walked, Jack remained solemn and to himself. They approached the bank and looked out at the mountain peaks in the distance.

"Wow, boys. What a view," Lito said. "The way these mountains come together. Man, it's beauty-full."

Meanwhile, the Bandits' eyes were also fixated on the sudden steep drop and whitecaps that went as far as the eye could see.

"All right, boys," Lito said. "This is Sugar Rush."

"Why do they call it Sugar Rush?" Gene asked.

"It's a lot of fun, pretty much; just a straight shot of adrenaline. Now, notice the river is pretty narrow in this section." Lito pointed down the river. "Really, the hardest part is right at the beginning here. It's about a twenty-foot drop in about forty yards or so. From the cliffs, the water is pushed in, and it's a lotta volume, especially with the water running high. Now, from that, you see that there?" Lito pointed to the water.

"Yeah, it kind of looks like it's boiling a little," Gene said.

"Exactly right, and it is. Ya fall in, and you're in hot water there." Lito laughed, but the boys didn't find the humor. Lito continued. "Anyway, there's a lotta water churning from the bottom, like a whirlpool, which makes the water not as buoyant. So, if we make it past that, all we do is go in the middle between the rocks. I think y'all will like this one."

"Hope you're right," Gene said.

Jack stayed uncharacteristically quiet.

"Okay, let's run back and get the canoe," Gene called.

Tiny ripples danced from under the canoe as it glided out into the water. Paddles cut through the current as the canoe squared up and headed toward the gap between the two cliffs. Gene's eyes continued to peel for the crazy snake and robbers while Edgar paddled away downstream. Jack, on the other hand, was thousands of miles away in his mind, sulking.

"All right, guys. Remember, look for the Vs between the rocks, and paddle straight. This is gonna be fun," Lito said.

Taking one last gaze at the cliffs that drifted behind him, Edgar looked up. He paddled as the sound echoed back to him. His eyes focused, the water dropped, the front of the canoe was in the air, suspended above the drop, and…

"Agh!" Edgar screamed. He held the paddle above his head while water pelted him in the face. Exhilarated, he smiled, crashing through cresting waves. Soaked, the canoe launched and continued its downstream drop.

"Woo-hoo!" Lito yelled, jumping from his seat.

Gene let go a loud, "WHOOP! This is fun!"

Itching to get into the action, Jack looked on, antsy, wanting to be the captain.

"Edgar. Hit the V!" Lito yelled. "Paddle right. Gene, counter paddle." Lito continued to yell as the four bounced in their seats. "Good job, boys! Just keep her straight now! Jack, keep your eyes open, buddy. We need ya, buddy."

Untouched through three hundred yards of whitewater, the Bandits cut through the water with ease. Lito spotted a downed tree in the water. Lito waited a few seconds for Jack to take the lead, but Jack mentioned nothing of it.

"Edgar, paddle to the right. Go right!" Lito yelled.

Abruptly Jack stood and tried to take matters into his own hands. "Edgar. Give it here. Give it here!" Jack wrestled the paddle from Edgar's hands.

They barreled down the river, full speed, on a crash course with a partially submerged tree. Jack's paddle cut through the water. His torso tightened. Stroke by stroke, the canoe moved to the right, but the tree got closer and closer. One last strong, firm paddle from Jack and—

Crack! A full speed collision. Edgar was ejected headfirst. His body slammed into the rock-filled water. Jack, disoriented, stood and looked on, followed by Gene and Lito. Floating to the surface, Edgar rolled over, his forehead bleeding, his body drifting down the rapids.

"Let's go. Let's go, boys!" Lito sounded a bit panicked.

The three tried to paddle, but the canoe didn't budge. The canoe was wedged between the two limbs of the tree, pressed on by thousands of pounds of water pressure. Jumping furiously, Lito, Gene, and Jack shimmied to try to free the canoe, but to no avail.

In the distance, Edgar slowly faded away.

"Oh, my god! Let me see." Lito ran to the front. "Oh, Lord, it's bad. We have to get out."

"We have to save Edgar!" Jack hollered. "Where the heck is he?"

Chapter 24
Remains Found

Pacing in circles inside the Mathias kitchen, Jack's and Gene's parents waited nervously for a call from the police about the whereabouts of their children.

"I don't know." Gene's mom swiped tears from her eyes. "Where could they be? I just can't believe it."

"Yeah, I can't believe it either." Jack's mom picked at her nails. "I knew he was upset about summer school, but I never thought he'd do anything like this."

Cathy's phone rang. Sprinting to the table, Gene's mom picked up her phone, fumbled with it, and answered. "Hello?"

"Yes, this is Local Sheriff Eldridge. Is this Gene Henderson's mom, Mrs. Cathy Henderson?"

"Yes, it is. It is," she said, almost popping out of her skin.

"Oh, good. I wanted to call you because we found some remains along the trail," Sheriff Eldridge said. Gene's mom dropped the phone and fell to the floor.

"Hello? Hello? Hello?" Sheriff Eldridge asked, worried.

Gene's stepdad picked up the phone. "Hello?"

"Phew. I thought I was going to have to call an ambulance and save the day. Anyway, I didn't finish. We found some remains along the trail, an old fire with a marshmallow wrapper, crackers, and some chocolate. Then upstream from there we found a garden, a tent-like thing, a high wire, and other stuff. Would any of that be from your son?"

"Umm, they left two days ago, so I'm sure the s'mores stuff is theirs, but not the other things," Gene's stepdad said.

"Hmm. Yeah, kinda what we expected. Well, we found some evidence, and the man's name is Lito Linden. We believe there's a possibility he's armed and dangerous. Anyway, at this given point in time—given by me, by the way—I expect them to be in the canyon portion of the Gauley, so we may not be able to reach them until they float downstream or use other means."

"The Gauley," Gene's stepdad said. "That's a dangerous place."

Jack's mom gasped.

"But trust me," the sheriff said. "We will get your son out alive. And I will personally guarantee that. The man who has them kidnapped lives savagely, and we are prepared to take him out at all costs," Sheriff Eldridge concluded, matter-of-factly.

"Oh, okay. Well... thank you, Sheriff, and I know you will," Gene's stepdad said.

"Oh, yeah, trust me. Nothing goes on under my watch. Other than this one freckle." Sheriff Eldridge laughed.

"Yeah, yeah, um… Okay, well, I don't know what to say. Except Jack's parents are here also. I'll fill them in. Let us know if you hear more. Bye." Gene's stepdad hung up with a puzzled look on his face.

Jack's parents, with their arms crossed, stared at Gene's stepdad. Cathy sobbed into her hands.

"Um—yeah." Gene's stepdad nodded, holding in emotion. "I think everything is going to be fine."

Jack's parents remained frozen with their arms crossed.

Chapter 25
All Tied and Tangled

Jack looked on as Lito's strong, weathered hands latched on to the side of the canoe as he stepped onto the submerged tree. He slipped but caught his balance on the bouncing limb. Armed and dangerous, he grabbed a paddle with his right hand.

"All right, Jack, step out here," Lito yelled over the rushing current.

Jack's feet cut through the rushing water onto the flimsy limb. Cold, slippery, and battling the current, his feet slipped, his shins cramped, as he grasped on to the canoe to keep from getting stuck or washing away in the current.

"All right, Gene, you stay in the back of the canoe. Now, Jack, you see how it's caught between the two branches here?" Lito said to Jack, pointing into the water.

"Yeah," Jack said.

"I want you to grab this here paddle." Lito handed him another paddle. "We're both gonna wedge them between the canoe and tree branches." Lito wedged his side. "Now you do the same on your side."

Jack pushed the paddle flush between the canoe and tree.

Lito shouted to Jack over the current. "Now, we're both gonna slowly—slowly is the key word—press down on the paddle. It should create a ramp and shoot out over this thing. Now, these paddles don't have much tolerance, though, so don't push hard or the weight of the canoe and current will break the wood in half. Also, be prepared to jump on when this frees. 'Cause it'll be truckin'."

"I got it. I got it, Lito!" Jack yelled. "Let's do it. Ready? One, two, three!"

The two groaned. Their muscles and veins bulged. They pushed the oars firmly against the canoe and lifted slowly. Impatiently Jack torqued, expediting the process.

Crack. Falling, Jack's left hand latched to the side of the canoe. He regained balance and looked at his right hand, with only a two-foot piece of paddle remaining.

"My gosh, Jack, no!" Lito yelled. "Jeez. What did I tell ya? You can't fight it. Now that's a problem. Might as well make that piece driftwood."

Jack, frustrated and dejected, wound up and was about to throw the piece into the water, but stopped. He glanced at its sharp ends and realized it was like a knife. *Yet small enough to conceal.* Jack reached under the front of the canoe and stowed it away.

"All right, Jack. Quick, grab the other paddle. If you break this one, we got no chance getting outta here. I'll tell ya that."

"Take it easy, Jack," Gene said. "Do what Lito said."

Jack shoved the paddle between the tree and the canoe.

"Gently, Jack. Smooth. This time, push toward the handle more," Lito said.

The canoe freed itself from the tree, slid up the oars, and came straight toward Jack and Lito.

"Hold on to the paddle and roll into the front!" Lito yelled.

Jack and Lito tumbled into the front while the canoe shot rapidly down the river. They quickly shot up and paddled from their knees as the whitewater caps drenched and filled the inside of the canoe.

"Good job," Gene said.

"Keep paddlin'," Lito yelled.

Their water-filled canoe flopped through the last set of rapids and approached the last obstacle, a twenty-foot waterfall.

"Paddle, Jack. Paddle. Okay, now stop!" Lito yelled, as he thrust one last stroke into the water. "Hold on to your seats!"

The three screamed.

Gene's eyes closed while Jack and Lito lay down like they were in a winter bobsled. They launched off the falls. Gene's pants soaked before the first splash.

"WHOA!" Jack blurted.

Splash! The front of the canoe pierced through the water, and water filled the canoe.

"Gene. Gather the stuff!" Lito yelled.

"Let's get to Edgar!" Gene yelled.

Jack and Lito swam a straight line toward Edgar. Gene, shivering, latched to the water-filled canoe and rounded up all of their floating items before kicking to shore.

Jack and Lito reached Edgar. His face was bloody and off colored, but his head was upward and out of the water. Lito grabbed behind his head, and Jack placed his hand behind his back and swam to shore.

Edgar didn't move.

"Edgar. Ya hear me, bud? Edgar," Lito said. He lightly slapped Edgar's face. "Edgar, you in there?"

Edgar's eyes twitched and fluttered open. His stomach pushed out, and his body contorted.

"Roll his head over, Lito. He has to cough," Jack called out.

Jack and Lito rolled Edgar over as he violently coughed out water.

"It'll be all right, man." Jack tried to comfort his friend. "Just keep coughing."

Moments passed, the coughing stopped, and Edgar's skin brightened up. Dazed but fully conscious, he sat up.

Gene dashed over with a canteen of spring water from his bag. He poured it on Edgar's bloody face. The red blood washed away, and the root of the cut was revealed.

Lito assessed the wound. "Wow, not too bad actually. You, my friend, are fortunate. That could have been a whole lot worse. Just take it easy for a minute,

Edgar. Have some of this." Lito handed him a canteen of water.

Edgar could barely speak. He tried but could only nod.

While Edgar recovered, Lito, Jack, and Gene dumped out the water from the canoe and shook out the waterlogged bags.

"Soaked," Jack said, not exactly thrilled.

"You're telling me. Hopefully this stuff dries out by tonight," Gene said.

"Well, ya know why this all happened?" Lito asked.

"Why?" Jack responded

Lito pointed at Jack. "You were the communicator. You shoulda called it. But rather than be a part of the team, ya chose to sulk. All about Jack, ain't it?" Lito yelled.

"What do you mean?" Jack shot back. "First off, I should have been the captain. Don't know why I was in the middle. And I tried to avoid it and paddled as hard as I could."

"Well, rather than fighting with Edgar over the paddle, maybe you should've let him have it, and trusted he could do it. Maybe. We got three people working together going downstream. Yet one person wants to be the hero and go upstream. You're like a wild mustang, Jack. You got all the potential in the world, but if you don't join us, what good are ya for us?" Lito hollered.

Jack grabbed his wet bag from the ground and looked at Edgar and Gene. "Come on, guys. Let's go.

We're not far from where the cave is. Let's just go back home. Had enough of this guy." Jack gave Lito a dirty look.

Jack hiked up the trail while Edgar, Gene, and Lito huddled and talked things over.

"Ya know, Jack ain't helping us with this kind of attitude," Lito whispered.

"Yeah, I know, but trust me, he's very stubborn," Gene said. "Not sure he's going to come back."

Jack looked back when he heard what Gene said. But he said nothing and kept walking.

"Wait, Jack!" Gene called.

Turning around, Jack yelled, "What?"

"I think we should keep going," Gene said. "We've come this far."

"Why? For what?" Jack said.

"Y-Yeah," Edgar said. "B-Bandits. We're th-the Bandits."

That got to Jack a little. But not enough to turn down the trail.

"Come on," Gene called. "We did plan on staying another day. And I'll admit, a lot of things have sucked, but walking back could maybe suck just as much—and for what? Nothing to show for it. Actually, why is it me saying this and not you? We're, like, trading places," Gene said.

Lito stepped in. "He's saying it because things ain't going his way. When I met you the other day, you reminded me of a friend I had. I loved him but he was the same way. When things didn't go his way, he'd quit. Never got him very far."

Jack walked back toward them. "I'm not quitting. I just don't like being told what to do. So, I want to quit, and I can."

"Jack, you're right, you can quit. And that is fine and there is nothin' wrong with that. But life throws a lotta quitting things at ya. Things don't always go your way. So truly, do you want that treasure?" Lito asked.

"I don't know?" Jack shrugged and stared at a hole in the ground.

"It's a simple yes or no, Jack. Do you want that treasure?"

Glancing at the ground, then to Lito, Jack nodded and said, "Yes."

Lito cracked a smile. "I thought so. So, if you really want it, it ain't gonna fall out of the sky. Wouldn't that be nice? Heck, it'd be so easy. Everyone would have whatever they want. You have to face the pain and all the pitfalls, or ya won't enjoy the reward. If ya really want it, it's there." Lito pointed down the river. "Just go out and get it. 'Cause if you pass on a dream now, it'll just be easy to say dreams are dreams your whole life. And you'll probably surround yourself with plenty of people that'll make you feel you're right about that."

Jack walked back to the group. "Let's go get that treasure." He smiled at Lito.

Lito patted his back. "You're a good man, Jack."

The three huddled up, away from Lito, to discuss the possibilities.

Inside the huddle, Gene said, "Jack, I know you. You will never live this down if you don't get this treasure, and you know it. It'll really annoy me more to hear about it for three hundred and sixty-five consecutive days than to just suck it up for the next five hours or so and risk being killed by massive rapids we don't belong on. But I want to. For you, and a slight bit of getting the gold, too."

The three laughed.

"Okay, but I like being in charge. Lito is kind of being a buzzkill, you know? What do you think, Edgar?" Jack said.

"I s-say g-go for…"

Click. Bang! A gunshot.

"Freeze. Hands up."

The Boonetown Bandits' arms shot to the sky. They glanced at each other but were too afraid to look at who fired the gun.

Thoughts exploded through their heads. *How could Lito turn on us? What is going on? Who else would be here? Is it the men from before? Did the gunshot kill Lito?*

"Hands high where I can see them," the man said.

Gene's eyes focused and locked, tunneling in at the gun. It was much larger than the last one, and chrome. He took a deep breath.

206

Jack's heart raced. *Is this real? Should I kick him? He has a gun.* Jack stared across to another man with unsightly chest hair and watched him hog-tie Lito.

"You boys escaped the cave," Johnny said. "But you don't quit, do ya? Johnny's not so nice this time. Hey there, Jackie boy. I'm gonna tell your daddy." Johnny let out a cynical laugh.

Kicking the dirt and clenching his fists, Jack tried to compose himself, but all he wanted to do was attack the man.

"So, have you guys ever heard of the saying, 'hitting rock bottom'?" Johnny asked and followed it with another belly laugh. Johnny and Bruno tied the Bandits up and forced Edgar on Johnny and Bruno's raft to paddle, and Jack, Gene, and Lito into the canoe.

"See ya later, alligator," Johnny said. He pushed the canoe into the water. Then he and Bruno hopped onto their raft they had tied to the canoe. "Let's go for a ride," Johnny called.

The canoe and raft floated down the Gauley. In the canoe dragging behind, Jack sat in the front, Gene in the middle, and Lito at the back. Ropes were tied tightly around their wrists and ankles, cutting off circulation. The large rocks tied to their feet rolled over their toes each time the canoe swayed.

"Jack, quit moving, man," Gene whispered. "My toenails are turning purple."

"You should've put on shoes," Jack jabbed back. "But this does suck. I'm going to figure something out, trust me. Just give me some time."

Lito squirmed and wrestled with the ropes.

The big raft dragged through the water, slowly pulling the canoe along. Johnny and Bruno joked and laughed while playing cards on a small, wobbly card table with a box of cereal on the end.

"Yo, Edgar. If you paddle any slower, we'll all die of old age," Johnny said. "I'm not dying today, only you guys." Johnny laughed as Bruno joined in with a loud, obnoxious laugh that sprayed cereal all over Johnny's face.

"What the heck, you slobbin' pigface! Did your mom not teach you any etiquette? Jeez!" Johnny scolded Bruno, as he wiped off his face.

Edgar dripped with sweat as he paddled the float down the river. Draped over the front of the canoe, he transitioned from left to right, grimacing each time.

"You know, Edgar," Bruno said. "I remember last time we beat up your brotha, you looked like a beached whale on your bed. It took us pummeling your brotha to finally put your chips down. Maybe we can be your weight-loss system. You may not be as plump and portly." Bruno and Johnny laughed.

Clenching the paddle, Edgar gritted his teeth and lifted his paddle slowly out of the water. He took a deep breath before forcefully plunging his paddle deep into the water and continued paddling.

Lounging in his chair, Johnny pulled out a bag, unzipped it, and revealed a gun. He brought it to his mouth, bit into it, and put it away.

"Man. You guys see that? He's freakin' nuts," Jack said, whipping his neck around to Gene and Lito.

Lito shook his head and said, "Jeez. That ain't right. Guess Edgar's sweating bullets and soon Johnny will be—"

Gene interrupted, "Yeah, I saw him eat a cigarette earlier. These guys aren't right."

"He ate a cigarette?" Jack asked. "That's almost as stupid as smoking one. Man, that's crazy."

Johnny unfolded the map on the card table and looked over it. Bruno joined in, looking at the map. Johnny spoke in a loud whisper. "So, about one more meander, and we got the rapids. Maybe half mile, tops. There should be two rapids, but they're close togetha. I'm thinking we drop them in at the top. That way their bodies sink, and nobody's gonna find 'em in these rapids. We can then take their, um... canoe. Sound like a plan, Bruno?"

"That sounds like a plan. You sure we don't wanna keep any of the kids? We do need kids. That Jack, we could take 'em with us. Bet they could sell a lotta stuff for us. What ya think?" Bruno asked.

Glancing at Jack sitting in the canoe, smiling, Johnny scratched his chin.

"Nah, leave 'em for the fishes. That kid, there's somethin' about him. He just always has that grin, like he's up to something. Sweet kid, I'm sure, but I dunno."

"Yeah, you're probably right. Hey, you gettin' hungry?" Bruno called to the boys in the canoe. "You wanna eat? Maybe we can give the kids a last request quick and grab a bite. Whaddya say?" Bruno asked.

Johnny nodded his head and yelled, "Hey, kids. You got one last request? What do ya wanna do? The rapids are rapidly"—Johnny laughed and winked—"approaching." Jack turned around and whispered, "Let's take a pee on the shore." Jack winked at Gene.

Gene, having confidence in Jack's plan, yelled back, "We want to pee on the shore."

Johnny responded, "The kids spoke. They gotta pee. Don't think about waterfalls."

"Ya heard your friends, Edgar. Over there." Bruno pointed to the shore.

Paddling slowly toward the shore, Edgar's muscles ached and quivered, and the grimace hardened on his face as his brow wrinkled and dripped sweat.

Jack bent down and grabbed the long, sharp shaft he had hidden under the front of the canoe. He gingerly tucked it into the bottom of his pants, extending from the knee all the way down to the shoe. Prepared for a showdown, his heart raced, and adrenaline pumped. He focused in on the men, watching and listening to learn any more tells before the fight for their lives started.

Finally, the Edgar-powered barge made it to shore. Johnny took Edgar to land while Bruno untied Gene and Jack and escorted them to shore. Lito stayed in the canoe. After trudging through river mud, Gene and Jack walked through the tall grass on the bank to a bush. As they prepared to pee behind a tree, Johnny watched Edgar as Bruno talked and glanced to make sure Jack and Gene were in sight. Jack and Gene looked forward, and Jack had an epiphany.

Jack whispered to Gene, "All right, I was going to attack them. But look, Gene, at the bush, and hold your pee quick."

Gene looked. "The berries?"

"Yeah, aren't they the kind that can give people bad diarrhea?" Jack asked.

"That's one of many things they can give you. Why?" Gene tried to follow Jack's logic.

"We're going to put them in their cereal. They plan on eating quick. So, here's the deal. I'm going to say I have to go number two. You're going to carry them back and put them in the cereal box," Jack said with a grin.

"Why do I have to carry them back? Why can't I have to go number two?" Gene asked.

"You want to live, right?" Jack asked.

Jack and Gene whistled away on the berries until Gene called out, "I have to go number two, guys."

All Jack could do was glare at Gene.

Gene walked farther into the woods.

Defeated, Jack picked the freshly peed on berries from the tree and concealed them in his hand. Walking back, Johnny muted his cell phone and yelled, "Hey, Jack, just hang out on the raft! I'll be right out."

Stepping onto the float, Jack spotted the cereal box. Looking up at the bank, he saw Johnny's head turn, and Jack's hand slowly and quietly snuck its way into the crinkly-wrapped cereal bag. Johnny's head turned back. Jack pulled his hand away just in time.

"What are you doing?" Lito whispered.

"Shhhhh, you'll see."

Jack looked back to shore again in time to see Johnny looking straight at him. Jack waved and smiled, and Johnny went back to talking on the phone. Jack opened the crinkly bag and dropped the berries inside and closed the box.

"This is going to be great," he whispered to Lito.

Minutes later, the raft rocked as the four stepped back on, and once again they set sail. Johnny instructed Jack and Gene to sit on the floor of the float until they finished their cereal, while Edgar paddled.

"Hey, any of ya kids want any of this, huh?" Johnny asked.

Gene and Jack looked at each other. "Um, no, thanks."

"Sh-Sure," Edgar said.

Jack looked at Edgar. "No, you don't, man. You don't like that kind of cereal, remember?"

"Yeah," Gene said. "You hate it."

212

"Don't know what ya missin'," Bruno said.

Johnny rooted through his things and pulled out a large Ziploc bag. "Well, here, you three can be our test group. You gotta tell me if you like these candy cigarettes we sell. Also try these delicious chocolate guns." Johnny handed them the candy cigarettes before pulling out a chocolate gun that looked incredibly real. "Now, this is our number one seller! Gene, bet you remember this thing, don't ya? Looks pretty real, don't it?" Johnny spun the gun's revolver.

"So, wait," Jack said. "You guys sell this stuff? Does it shoot?"

"Well, it only shoots jelly beans for now. We're workin' on the chocolate's density so it can fire live rounds, and that way, we can eat the evidence after the crime. But it's a sore subject at the moment."

"Wow! How do you make it look so real?" Jack followed up.

"Now that's a better question, Jackie boy! Cause we're the best! We got the biggest underground pipeline in the country. We have the whole east and west coast distribution. It would be easier just to sell in stores, but it's illegal, so we gotta do it black market. It's these parents nowadays, they're just so over-sensitive, even though their kids are constantly killing each other on these games. The way I see it is, a little candy's not killing anyone, right? So, we gotta keep it under wraps. And we import the sugar from banned countries. But, to look at the bright side, even if it was legal, taxes on these

213

things would be through the roof! The government wants it all, and then some," Johnny said.

Gene and Jack took a bite. "Not bad," Jack said.

"Pretty good actually," Gene added.

"Y-Yeah," Edgar agreed.

Lito declined sampling the candy, saying, "Sugar ain't good for ya."

"But why would you guys' plan to kill us then? If you're not about killing and stuff?" Gene asked.

"Honestly, we don't wanna. We love kids," Johnny said sincerely. "But one lie turns into another, and before ya know it, you're caught up in the world of crime. And in this par-ticula' situation, with the treasure, you knowing our names, we kinda have to. Then the cherry on top is Edgar boy here; his brotha's been stealing our business. Making molds and copyin' our products and trying to undercut our business. So, it's a handful a things. Hope you understand."

Jack looked ahead. "Yeah, well, you better finish your cereal. Those rapids are almost on us." He glanced at Gene and winked.

Crashing through the flakes, Johnny and Bruno scarfed their cereal.

"I'll tell ya what, Bruno, these berries are fresh. I mean, not only low in sodium, but fresh and…" Johnny looked closely at it. "There's actually two different berries. Check it out, Bruno," Johnny said, far more excited than most about cereal.

"Oh, yeah, it does." Bruno smelled a spoonful of berries. "Pretty fresh. You can tell, these berries were beside an asparagus patch. Smell, Johnny?"

Jack's body rocked the boat with all the laughter he held inside. "Eat up," Jack said with a chuckle.

Johnny and Bruno glanced at Jack, and then looked at each other. Johnny shrugged his shoulders and said, "Kid's right."

Chomping away, Johnny and Bruno shoveled spoonful after spoonful into their faces before pouring another bowl. Jack's cheeks were bright red, and they soon became sore from holding in laughter.

They floated along as the sound of the rapids grew ever closer. Five hundred yards ahead, the tree line dropped. Jack thought that he may need a plan B since no side effects had taken hold. He patted his leg where the makeshift knife was secured.

Suddenly there was a rumble, then the sound of a low-pitched tuba mixed with a touch of water in the chamber.

Farting.

"I'm-a-sorry, Bruno, I'm-a-not feelin' too well," Johnny said, holding his stomach, and hunching over.

"Me neitha," Bruno said.

Rounds of fiery, explosive farts echoed out of Johnny's backside cavern as the scorched chair below him toppled and his ribcage hit the floor. Crawling and vomiting his way to the side of the raft, Johnny burned like a two-wick candle at both ends.

Disoriented and sweating, Bruno stood and dry-heaved off the side, yet still kept his inner feelings secret.

"Good one," Lito said to Jack. "I knew you were a smart guy." Lito winked.

Amid the chaos, the noise of the rapids heightened to a roar. Jack glanced at Lito and pulled the long shaft from his pants. Lito nodded, and Jack mouthed, "Where should I put it?"

Lito motioned with tied hands at the floating barrels under the raft, and mouthed back, "Jam it in the bunghole."

Jack looked confused and put his hands out to the side. "Seriously?"

"Yeah, do it," Lito mouthed back.

Johnny was on all fours like a dog leaning over the front of the raft. Jack sprang into action. With the Bandits' and Lito's lives on the line, Jack, like an Olympian with a javelin going for gold, sent a missile just feet away, spiraling right into the...

"Agh!" Johnny screamed, with his eyes bulging out and a long shaft in his butt.

Lito shook his head in disbelief and yelled, "I meant the bunghole in the barrels under the raft!"

Suddenly Bruno grabbed Edgar and Gene, and then veered toward Jack's blindside with something in hand.

"Jack!" Lito yelled.

Johnny's stomach rumbled, and he let out a catastrophic fart, sounding like a rocket taking off from Cape Canaveral.

Johnny catapulted into the water, causing the raft's weight to shift. Bruno lost his balance as Edgar and Gene bit his hands. Bruno released the two boys and stumbled before falling on his head. The Bandits rolled a dazed and ill Bruno into the water.

Splash.

"Let's go, guys!" Jack yelled while Gene and Edgar jumped into the canoe.

Jack furiously untied Lito while looking toward the front of the canoe. The biggest rapids they had ever seen loomed in front of them. Meanwhile, Edgar and Gene untied the rope from the raft.

Lito was freed. He stood up and took charge. "All right, boys, this is Upper Shotgun! We're just gonna have to wing it. We'll scout out lower when we get there. Jack, you're the captain, take the back. Edgar, take the front. Gene and I can watch for rocks."

Then…

Blindsided.

A hand shot through the water and latched on to Lito's neck. Lito and Bruno fell into the middle of the canoe.

"Bruno's back!" Jack yelled.

Bruno sat on top of Lito with his strong hands around his neck. Lito gasped for air. Edgar jumped into action. Bruno's eyes met Edgar's. He let go of Lito.

A first-class rumble in the Gauley ensued.

"What ya gonna do? St-St-Stutter? You're just a big, fat beached whale," Bruno mocked.

Bruno went for the neck. Edgar threw a right blindside hook. And *bam*. Bruno didn't see that coming. Down went Bruno! Down went Bruno into the water and floated away.

Lito crawled back in his seat. "Thanks, dude!"

"N-No problem, I've b-b-been dreaming of that," Edgar said with a wide smile before taking a seat.

"Only five yards until drop off!" Lito called.

Chapter 26
Shotgun Falls

Staring out through the rising mist, Edgar looked down at the tops of trees, which resembled heads of broccoli at the bottom of the gorge. Shotgun Falls looked more like a large cliff with water falling off it than a river. Gasping at the scariest thing in his life, Edgar extended out over the edge first, his skin trembled, and then he fell.

"Agh!" all four screamed.

"We need a parachute!" Jack yelled, while the wind pulled his hair and skin back.

They fell thirty feet.

"Hold on to the sides, boys!" Lito yelled.

Splash!

Crashing into the water and cutting through the surface, the four, still inside the canoe, plunged underwater as the canoe became a submarine.

"BBAAHHAHH!" the four screamed underwater. Bubbles tickled their faces in their wooden submarine.

The front slowly rose up as the once-submerged canoe popped to the surface. They gasped when they came up. The four sucked in the precious oxygen.

"I feel like a wet muskrat!" Lito yelled.

Barely afloat and almost fully submerged, Lito looked around. "We'll shoot the rockslide right after this. This is the one with the keeper hole, ya know, the whirlpool thing. We gotta go right hard, but we can't with all this water in the boat. We're dead meat." Lito used his hands to bail water out of the canoe.

"Gene, help me. Edgar and Jack, take control!" Lito called.

The river narrowed and all currents pushed into a narrow slide not much wider than the canoe, before a steep drop spilled into a hard current, pushing into a keeper hole.

Jack paddled and called to Edgar, "Right, right!"

Narrowly missing the rock, the two continued.

"Edgar, paddle left!" Jack yelled, as Edgar nodded. "I'll counter. Go between the rocks!"

Shooting through the rocks approaching the slide, Lito and Gene worked tirelessly bailing out the water with their hands and the mini shovel Lito brought along. The canoe rose in the current with each ounce of water removed. The river narrowed as the rocks touched both sides of the canoe and…

"Hold on!" Jack yelled as they hit the slide.

The canoe picked up speed and hydroplaned across the water, reminiscent of a colossal speed slide at a water park. Their hair flapped in the wind, and water stung their faces. Coming into view as they got closer to the bottom was a drop-off, more current, and…

"Keeper hole! Jack, ya see that foam?" Lito yelled, holding on for dear life. "That's stuck there from the undercurrent; it won't escape. And if we go there, we won't either. Hard right off this dr—agh!" Lito was interrupted by the drop.

Splash!

The canoe glided across the water. They were headed full speed toward the rock wall and the keeper hole.

"Paddle backwards, Edgar!" Jack yelled as he countered and tried to stop the forward momentum away from the cliff and keeper hole. They were headed full speed at the dangerous obstacles. But suddenly, Jack's and Edgar's paddles displaced and pushed the water in perfect harmony. The canoe slowed. The back end spun around like a remote-controlled car and steered away from the cliff and keeper hole. Jack and Edgar had masterfully perfected the move.

Gene slowly raised his head from the floor and timidly peered over the side of the canoe, to his surprise. "Holy crap, you guys did it! Amazing!"

All four let out a sigh of relief, before they paddled to the bank to scout Lower Shotgun.

"Wow, Jack! Jeez, Edgar!" Lito glowed with excitement. "Y'all made me proud. I mean, that was pretty special."

"Thanks, man," Jack said. "But, we definitely wouldn't have made it without Edgar in the front."

Edgar cracked a smile. "Th-Thanks, Jack."

Jack and Edgar clicked their paddles together, and their smiles said it all. Afterward, they paddled and drifted along the bank with the canoe.

"Hold up, hold up. Bring it together, guys," Jack said to Lito and the Bandits.

All four put their hands together.

Jack yelled, "Lito and the Boonetown Bandits on three! One, two, three!"

"Lito and the Boonetown Bandits! Woo-hoo!"

Lito's crow's feet showed on the sides of his eyes, and his face shimmered in the sun.

Lito shook his head. "I'll tell ya what, boys. This has been a heck of a ride. I think you may have lit a fire inside me again. Y'all don't know what you do for me."

Jack, Gene, and Edgar gave Lito a hug and pats on the back.

"Yeah, guess we still got a rapid to do, then guess we can dig a—" Lito paused and listened intently. "Y'all hear that?"

Scanning the cliff and river upstream, they listened with eyes and ears for more clues. Two objects were flung off the upper waterfall above the rockslide.

"Oh, no! It's them. Let's get going quick," Jack said.

"Yeah, let's go!" Gene cried.

Edgar nodded.

"Nah, we can't go," Lito said, sympathetically. "There ain't no way they're gonna make it. They hit this, they're gonna drown."

"Hmm, that sucks," Jack said, putting his paddle in the water. "You guys ready?"

"Nah, guys, we better try to get them before they go into the keeper hole. They ain't never gonna make it, I mean it." Lito's eyes were heavy and red.

"Wait, the guys who killed Edgar's brother's friend possibly, and tried to kill us, we're going to save?" Jack asked.

"Wait, how do you know they killed him?" Gene asked.

"Just a guess, but probably not." Jack calmed.

Gene shook his head. "Well, anyways, sometimes Jack is crazy but not so much this time. You know, Lito, they did try to kill us, right?"

Lito shook his head. "Guys, sometimes y'all just have to turn the other cheek. And especially after what you did to his butt cheeks, Jack, and after what Edgar did to Bruno's cheek. Good punch by the way, Edgar," Lito said, giving Edgar a thumbs-up. "It don't matter; they ain't gonna be in a fighting mood. And don't matter who it is, I can't watch them drown. If we get them and they're feisty, we'll club 'em over the head like an ornery catfish."

Jack was just about to say something when Lito called out, "Here they come. Paddle out, boys!"

The grimacing men slid down the rockslide, like dead fish—belly up—before flipping head over feet off the falls.

Splash!

They violently torpedoed into the water. The men headed straight for the keeper hole, and the white foam approached, closer and closer until... The men were sucked in, like a ball of dust into a vacuum cleaner. Rotating, thrashing against the water, like dirty socks in a washing machine, the men dunked continuously, with only a split second of air on each upturn. Their bodies were ripped, stuck in a wash cycle that wouldn't stop.

Jack and Edgar paddled furiously toward the whirlpool. The stern floated around toward the men as their feet came to the surface every few seconds.

"All right, Jack, that's perfect. I'm gonna lean out, buddy, and grab 'em. When I do, paddle. And hey, Jack?" Jack and Lito locked eyes. "I'm proud of you, buddy. And honestly, I was hard on ya, 'cause I never had a son, but if I did, I'd hope he was just like you." Lito's eyes welled up. Jack nodded and his eyes went glossy as Lito patted him on his back, smiled and said, "The summer of Lito and the Bandits."

Lito wrapped his feet around the back of the stern seat and extended his arms. The back of the canoe was feet away from the dangerous current. Lito's hands opened for Johnny, who was in arm's reach. Johnny's arm moved, but not far enough.

"Dang," Lito said, outstretched off the back of the canoe. "Jack, if you could, buddy, come back about a half a foot."

With the slightest ease, Jack crept back, and the back of the canoe lowered and became wobbly from the current. Lito stretched out, and Johnny continued to circulate. Bruno, who hadn't come up, may have already been taken by the river. Lito's arm stretched as Johnny's head and hand came up. Lito grabbed ahold of Johnny's hand. The force torqued Lito down, and his feet unhinged from the canoe. Jack turned around in horror.

Splash!

"No!" Jack yelled.

Crashing into the water, Lito disappeared, ripped to the bottom. Jack scanned the water as the canoe floated toward the keeper hole.

The back of the canoe dipped down into the undertow. Jack looked down, stunned. He yelled, "Get to the front, Gene! Paddle, Edgar!"

Jack's eyes scanned the water for Lito while he paddled furiously. Lito's head surfaced.

"Jack, go!" Lito yelled before he was ripped to the bottom again.

Jack paddled, and the canoe broke free from the undertow. Jack looked back and Lito's head appeared.

"Believe!" Lito yelled, moments before being violently dunked under the water.

Finally, they were freed from the current.

Jack yelled to Edgar, "Stop!"

The three, with their hearts pounding, minds blurry, and stomachs turning terribly sour, stared at the water, but nothing came to the surface. They looked on, watching… waiting… waiting… wishing… Minutes passed, then hope. Ten more minutes passed…

The Bandits pulled the canoe onto the shore. They sat and watched and waited and waited some more, hoping Lito would reappear.

Staring hopelessly, a rainstorm hit their eyes. It was more of a typhoon while their bodies endured the crashing of a tidal wave. They felt like they were throwing punches under water. Their hearts, oh, so heavy, sank like a stone to the bottom. A friend, an adventure, closing. Sulking, with hands tightly pressed to their faces. Hours went by. The sound of the rapids reduced to a trickle in the background.

So many questions. Was this real? Was he gone? Would he come back? Was there a do-over? It was all replaced with the realization that Lito was gone. The truth stung. Lito was gone.

Chapter 27
Treasure the Moment

Hours passed. The deafening silence rang in their ears. The three sat along the bank. Jack noticed the sun sliding behind the evergreens to the west.

Jack stood and looked at his friends. "What would Lito want us to do? We're stuck on the side of a cliff, and still have to get to the bottom of the gorge."

"He'd want us to keep going," Gene said as he stood up.

Edgar nodded.

"That's right," Jack said. "And that's exactly what we're going to do." Jack lifted a canoe paddle to the darkening sky. "For Lito."

"For Lito," called Edgar and Gene.

"We have rapids to scout," Jack said, channeling his inner Lito.

Jack led the way to the end of a rock overlooking Lower Shotgun Falls. They noticed that, while not as long as the Upper Falls, there were still very technical spots.

"Do you guys see the way the water pushes after the first drop?" Jack pointed between the boulders in the water. "We have to hit that chute right after the drop. If we don't, we'll be kicked into another keeper on the left."

"W-We can d-do it," Edgar said.

Jack continued. "Now, after that we have to go left, and hmmm… That is just one big death trap of keeper holes wherever you go, isn't it?"

Gene grabbed ahold of the frames of his glasses and squinted. "Hmm… Yeah, really don't see any way around it. And with the water up, maybe it's just not passable, Jack?" Gene looked at Jack.

Edgar motioned with two thumbs pointing in the air. "N-No, Gene. Y-You're wrong. L-Let's jump it, like w-we did before."

Jack scratched his chin. "You know what, Edgar, we could. You're right. The same type of flow-rider boulder thing's in front of the keeper holes. If we go as fast as possible, we'll launch the boulder and jump over all the dangerous stuff. There's a chance. What do you guys think?" Their eyes darted between the distance needed to ramp the keeper hole and the wooden canoe.

"Yeah, our chances are maybe one in a hundred?" Gene figured.

"Really, that good?" Jack said excitedly. "Compared to the chances of your underwear getting caught on the deer's antlers, I say we do it. What do you think, Edgar?"

Edgar looked Jack dead in the eyes and raised his fist. "L-Let's do it."

The three huddled up.

"Let's do this for Lito," Jack said. "But the only thing is, we all have to believe, without a doubt. We can't afford to have someone not believing we can do this. Edgar, do you believe?"

"Yes," Edgar said clearly.

"Gene, what about you?"

Looking around, Gene was still showing doubt. He shuffled his feet and scratched the side of his neck while staring at the river. Wavering, Gene looked into the eyes of Edgar and Jack. Gene's shoulders raised. "All right, let's get this show rolling!" Gene cried. "For Lito, on three."

"One, two, three, for Lito!" the Bandits yelled.

Wasting no time, they jumped into the canoe and headed straight toward the first drop. Gene picked up the mini shovel and used it as a third paddle to give the canoe as much speed as possible.

"Remember, guys. Let's go off the right side of this drop, and then stay right, hit the V between the rocks, then ramp the rock to the treasure!" Jack said, his voice hitting a crescendo at the end.

The Bandits paddled with all their strength and all their hearts. When they approached the twenty-foot drop, Jack called out, "Edgar, paddle as hard as you can. Make your last stroke a strong one before we drop. That way we don't nosedive."

Paddling along, the front of the canoe leaned over the edge of the first drop. Edgar stroked the paddle, so strong, with strength pulling from deep inside his being.

Just seconds after, Jack gave one last full stroke, and they were airborne.

The three screamed while flying in the air. The canoe's front stayed level with the back until...

Splash! It was a perfect landing. Immediately paddles hit the water. Edgar paddled with determination. They sharply turned right. Jack counter-steered perfectly and Gene, with the shovel, gave it his all, too.

"Jeez, Gene. Put the shovel down. You're just splashing me in the face!" Jack yelled. Gene dropped the shovel and took on the communicator role.

"Paddle left, Edgar!" Gene yelled.

Flawlessly they shot through the rocks and crashed through the whitecaps. Locking in on the rock, Jack's eyes glowed red with fire and passion. Edgar, with a hunger far deeper than any cheese curl or chips could satiate, burned with conviction and belief. The Bandits glided toward the rock. One wrong move—one wrong anything—and game over. Anything less than eight feet of distance, and the three would be sucked up for eternity.

"Paddle, Edgar! Paddle like you never paddled before!" Jack yelled with a deep, unwavering voice, holding expectations to that of a seasoned paddler.

Stroke after stroke after stroke, Edgar's face turned redder and redder. One stroke after another after another, Edgar paddled, matching Jack's expectations.

Gene whispered to himself, "I think we can, I think we can, I think we can, I know we can..."

The canoe slipped up the rock at rapid speed, sending sparks where the canoe touched the bare rock. The three ramped the rock and took flight. They looked down and noticed the keeper hole was still in front of them. *Will it be enough?*

They reached their peak and descended toward the water. The hole still loomed underneath. Gene closed his eyes, praying. Edgar glanced down. Jack was still paddling in the air uselessly. They came down and *bam!*

Motionless, the three sat, noticing that they had indeed cleared the keeper hole. But so much so, that they over-ramped it by about two canoe lengths and landed on the rocky bank.

"Oh, jeez," Gene said, still grasping the shovel. "Well, we're on land! But the canoe is obliterated."

Jack stared at the useless pile of wood. He felt a twinge in his chest when he thought of Lito again. "He built this canoe and now it's gone. Like him."

Gene draped his arm around Jack's shoulders. "He'd be proud of us, man."

After several minutes of sitting in shock with the sun sliding behind the horizon line, the boys gathered their belongings. Exhausted from the day of paddling along and mourning Lito, the three settled down on their damp blankets, huddling up in the driest of the damp clothes. As the stars began to blink into place, they shared a quiet conversation.

"So, what are we going to do?" Gene asked, gazing at the stars.

"I don't know. I'm not even that worried about it for some reason," Jack said with a yawn.

"Yeah." Gene yawned. "Night, guys."

"Night," Jack said.

"N-Night," Edgar chimed in as the three, exhausted and numb, dozed off into a deep, deep sleep.

They awoke to loud cicadas and birds chirping in a natural symphony.

"Oh, my god!" Jack yelled. "Please. Shut up, birds! Figure it out already. For God's sake. Jeez."

"Yeah, you're right," Gene said. "They're out in full this morning. Guess they can feel the summer solstice coming."

"My back is killing me." Jack slowly stood, groggy. He held his back. "Did the ground hurt your backs?"

Gene and Edgar stretched.

"No, I'm good," Gene said. "How about you, Edgar?"

"I'm g-good," Edgar said.

Jack picked up his sleeping bag and stomped on the ground. "I slept on a rock, that's why."

Gene looked a little closer. "I don't think that's a rock." He kicked it. "I think it's a tree stump." Bending down, Gene moved residual dirt away and noticed old wood grains.

"Jack, the wood looks a lot like the wooden chest we found the map in. Remember?" Gene asked.

Jack looked closer. "Edgar, get me that shovel. We're going to find out."

Digging around the object, a very similar chest began to appear. Jack dug the remainder out. "Guys, come here. Help me pull this out…" Jack waved the other two over.

Pulling, the three slid the chest out of the ground. Their faces lit up.

"I can't believe it. It's got to be the treasure! Who wants to open it?" Jack asked.

"You can open it, man. Just in case," Gene said.

"Well, if it's a bomb, just know, you two are probably dead, too, so I'm only opening it if you stay right beside me," Jack said.

"Just open it already," Gene yelled.

With their eyes locked on to the chest they longed for—and had risked death for many times—Jack pulled on the rickety, old latch, but the lodged dirt had it stuck. Prying with his fingers, he pulled and pulled, and *snap*. Falling on his butt, Jack sat with the snapped latch in his hand.

"Jeez. You broke it," Gene joked.

The Bandits inched closer to the chest. Jack placed his hand on it, feeling the ridges of the wood grain. Slowly he pulled open the lid. A blinding shimmer of light shot out and emanated like a ray of sunshine from the opening of the chest. A tingling feeling warmed the boys as their dreams unfolded before their eyes. Opened for the world to see, the contents of the chest shone: two hundred, maybe even three-hundred-year-old treasure, with thousands of pieces of gold, jewels, and pearls. The gold shimmered like brand new, while the pearls shone like they were shaped from the deepest parts of the sea. The jewels radiated an array of colors.

Gene and Edgar, fixated, put their hands through the large pile of jewels. They stared blankly, with a perma-grin, while the riches fell through their hands. Looking to the right, Gene saw a note and picked it up.

"Wow," Gene said. "This is in the tribe's writing. The Shawnee wrote differently than us. It kind of looks like hieroglyphic stuff." Gene looked over it in appreciation.

"I don't understand," Jack said. "What do the Shawnee have to do with this treasure?"

Gene looked over the note. He definitely couldn't read it, but he said, "Maybe they found it and decided to leave it as an offering. But that doesn't mean we have to."

"Guess not," Jack said. But his heart didn't feel good. Instead of being filled with joy, Jack was feeling something else. It wasn't bad, but the treasure wasn't quite as thrilling as he thought it would be. But he was proud of the accomplishment and what they'd done.

Meanwhile, Gene's and Edgar's hearts raced. They did it. They had, right before them, the dream of almost every kid. It was like being warmed by a tropical sun after a long, dark, snowy winter. They had finally reaped the rewards of their hard work. All the pain took a back seat as the jewels shone, shone, oh, so bright, so...

"Wow! It's like ancient crypto, but you can actually touch it!" Gene admired.

Slam! Jack closed the lid. A dark cloud covered the rising sun.

"Jack. Why did you close it?" Gene asked. "I thought you'd be dancing." Gene and Edgar shot confused looks at each other.

Jack stepped between Gene and Edgar and the treasure.

"Wait, you're not going to get all selfish and try to keep it all? That's something you would do," Gene said.

Jack shook his head, frustrated. "You know what, guys? This is awesome, but I don't even care about it anymore."

Gene and Edgar stepped back.

"What are you talking about?" Gene asked. "This whole thing was your big goofy plan, right from the beginning. You wanted this treasure. Remember all the stuff you wanted to buy?"

"So what?" Jack said. "Sure, we can buy stuff. Cool. We'll buy stuff." Jack opened the chest and took a handful of gold coins out, holding them up. "Sure, this is great, but can this buy, oh, I don't know, just stupid stuff. Stuff we don't need! We had the adventure; that's really what it's all about!"

Gene looked at Edgar and then back to Jack. "Jack, are you freaking serious?" Gene said, shaking his head furiously. "Did a multidimensional alien shapeshift into your body? Are you behind those eyes?" Gene walked toward Jack, staring directly into his eyes.

Jack's head tilted back. "Yeah, I am. Why? It's a new me!"

Gene opened up the treasure and pulled out a gold coin, holding it up to Jack's face. "Do you know this one coin is worth like ten thousand dollars?" Gene waved it like a hypnotist in front of Jack's face. "And there's like ten thousand more of these inside of the chest, along with other priceless things."

Jack's pupils widened before he grabbed Gene's wrist and then took the gold coin out of his hand.

Jack held up the coin. "I can't exchange this for all we did and went through to get here! I can't exchange this to get to know Edgar or meet people like Lito!" Jack screamed to the sky, before looking back to Gene and Edgar. "Gene. Sure, the treasure got us here, but this just brought us together. The true treasure was this whole trip. Not this gold coin."

Jack grabbed several more gold coins from the treasure chest and began to wind up to throw the coins into the river.

Edgar and Gene waved their hands and yelled simultaneously, "No, Jack! Don't do it! Don't do it!"

Jack stopped. He turned away from the river and looked to Gene and Edgar. "Sike!"

Jack's teeth shone as he laughed. "You think I'm an idiot? Sure, the adventure was awesome, and all those stupid, cheesy sayings are actually true, surprisingly! But…"

Gene and Edgar listened intently.

Jack put his arms in the air. "This treasure makes things a whole heck of a lot better! Wooo! Let's party!"

The Boonetown Bandits erupted into a full-blown dance party. Jack started it off by making it rain with gold coins while Gene and Edgar helped themselves to the jewelry.

From olden day dances of Walk Like an Egyptian, The Carlton, and Macarena, to the Whip and Nae Nae, Floss and several more dances yet to be invented, the Bandits partied it up.

Gene showed a side few had seen. "Guys, check it out. Make it rain! Make it rain!" Gene sang with shiny necklaces draped around his neck and gaudy gold rings on his fingers. "I'm yo mane, G-Pain! I'm yo mane, I'm yo mane!"

Edgar then busted out dancing between Gene and Jack. He mumbled with his lips closed, "Ch-Ch-Check it out. I g-got grills."

Gene and Jack looked at Edgar's mouth.

Edgar smiled, revealing a mouth full of gold coins.

Gene and Jack laughed.

"Edgar, they didn't have toilet paper back then, they wiped their butts with their hands!" Jack said.

Edgar coughed. Gold coins flew from his mouth as he furiously spat them out down the bank and into the water.

Jack and Gene danced while Edgar gargled his mouth in the river. The party continued for a few more minutes before...

237

Low bass noise in the distance.

"Wait, stop! What's that noise?" Gene asked.

"Yeah, I hear it," Jack said, looking around. "It's humming. It feels like something's vibrating."

The three, frozen, listened for a few more seconds, and their faces began to resemble actors in a horror movie.

"The Shawnee gods!" Jack yelled. "They want their treasure back."

"Agh!" the three screamed and ran in circles aimlessly.

"Hurry! Put the gold back in the chest!" Gene yelled, while the Bandits' reactions resembled a mix of a chicken with its head cut off and a squirrel burying nuts.

Edgar and Gene frantically threw the gold back into the chest before Jack buried it.

"It's getting louder," Gene said, looking over his right shoulder.

"The trees are even starting to blow!" Jack screamed.

Jack threw on one last scoop of dirt while Gene and Edgar swiftly packed the dirt to hide any evidence. The Bandits ran as hard as they could and took shelter under a wide oak tree. The leaves shook violently, and the wind cut across the surface of the water and rippled it outward. Suddenly the Shawnee gods talked. In a strong voice, almost like out of a megaphone, from the sky, they said, "Anyone down there?"

The three looked at each other.

"What should we say?" Jack said. "I don't know what to do."

"Is this happening?" Gene asked. "Gods only talk from the sky in, like, movies. What is going on?"

"Oh, my god, guys, look!" Jack pointed at the ground. "It's casting a shadow. You see?"

Gene looked up. "It's flying? It's a—"

"It's an ancient alien," Jack said.

Turning away from Jack, Gene walked out from the trees and waved his arms.

"It's a helicopter, guys. Probably looking for us," Gene said.

"We're here to take you home," the helicopter pilot said. "You guys all right?"

Gene gave the okay sign. Jack and Edgar cheered.

"Move back. I'm going to land in the flat spot here."

The helicopter slowly lowered and touched down. Two men rushed out and brought the three into a windy, open area, and then into the helicopter. The men buckled them into their seats and gave them each a big green headset. Now, that was cool.

As the helicopter took off, the boys looked down at the Great Gauley.

"I'll never forget it," Jack said.

"Me neither," Gene murmured.

Edgar wiped tears from his eyes. Jack leaned over as far as he could with the seat belt locking him down. "It's okay, man. We all feel that way about losing Lito."

Glancing down at the countless trees dancing in the wind below, Jack noticed something from his window seat. He did a double take. Something was in the tree. Jack rubbed his eyes and looked again. He waved. "It's Lito! Hey, guys, look! Come here, it's Lito!" Jack yelled, bouncing out of his seat and pounding on the glass.

Edgar and Gene looked down.

"Wait, where did he go? He was just there," Jack said.

Gene and Edgar, rather than saying anything, gave him a pat on the back and left it at that.

The helicopter headed back to the town. As they approached the airport hangar, they noticed the field was filled with cars, people, and different local news station trucks. Little did the boys know they were about to become famous.

Chapter 28
Rescued

The men helped the boys out of the helicopter. With shaky knees, they walked into the hangar where they were greeted by their loved ones.

"Genie!" Gene's mom yelled, crying. She and his stepdad embraced him.

"Jack. Jack! We missed you!" Jack's mom gave him a big hug.

"I'm glad you're okay, Edgar." Jack's and Gene's parents hugged Edgar like their own.

Principal Kinsey even greeted Jack with a wide smile. "Jack, I'm glad you're okay. We were all worried sick." Kinsey patted Jack on the back before stepping away. "Listen, Jack, if you want to delay summer school a few weeks, by all means, it's fine by me!"

Jack smiled. A shimmer of light glistened from his eyes. "You know what, Mr. Kinsey? After almost dying, I'm actually looking forward to summer school." Jack put out his hands. "Death or summer school? Hmm... I'll take summer school!"

The two laughed while Mr. Kinsey put his hand on Jack's shoulder.

"All right, you win, Jack. See you tomorrow," Kinsey said with a wink. Minutes later, stepping outside into the crowd, the Bandits were greeted by flashbulbs, television cameras, and people everywhere. Everyone wanted to know how the three missing kids survived the kidnapping by America's Most Wanted Criminals. On the helicopter, the Boonetown Bandits decided to never mention the treasure. They told their folks the trip was just an adventure and nothing more.

"Excuse me, Jack. I'm a spokesperson for Channel Six news. Do you mind being interviewed?" a fancily dressed woman asked Jack.

"Um, sure. Don't mind at all," Jack said.

"We're coming to you live from Channel Six, Boonetown. I am Joan Morgan here with the young Jack Mathis," the reporter said.

"Um, it's Mathias, not Mathis," Jack said.

"Oh, okay," the reporter whispered in Jack's ear. "Sorry." The reporter went on. "How did you feel, lost in the woods, with a killer like Lito looming?"

"Um, Lito wasn't a killer. I think maybe Johnny 'Soft Hands' and Bruno were. But not Lito," Jack said.

"Okay, so wait. This Lito guy. I mean, wow, what a manipulator. So, this guy may have been known as Johnny 'Soft Hands' and Bruno 'The Bull'? Like he had a tri-personality? I mean, how heinous, right?"

"Um, no. No, they were separate people. Lito was good, the other two were bad. Pretty simple, you know?" Jack said.

"No, I don't know," the reporter said. "Okay, so how traumatized were you and—well, are you? I mean, what was the most traumatizing part in the whole ordeal? You're probably wrecked for life, right?"

Knowing full well the reporter wanted a show, Jack figured he should entertain. "Well, you know, an anaconda latched ahold of me in the water. I fought him off, and then put him in a sleeper. Then we were chased by at least a three-thousand-pound grizzly bear. And, honestly, I got tired of running from him, so I just turned around and killed him with my bare hands. Killed him. Right on the spot. We skinned him and used his fur for blankets."

"Wow, Jack! That's just—wow!" the reporter said while gazing into the camera and giddily holding the microphone. "I mean, an anaconda and a three-thousand-pound grizzly bear. That could be a record, Jack. I mean, pull up the breaking news on the bottom of the screen. Dara, at the news desk, please pull up the breaking news. Three-thousand-pound grizzly bear in Boonetown. All right, thanks, Jack, for your time." The reporter walked away without allowing Jack to get a last word.

As the camera panned away, Jack could only hear and see flashbulbs and people, along with the reporter in the background. Through the crowd and flashbulbs, Jack saw something shining twice as bright in the distance, waving. His world stopped. All noise was silenced, and a sound of a kick drum was beating out of his chest.

Bump, bump, bump. Jack's heart pounded.

Sarah Sharp ran toward him. Like two lovebirds flying through a meadow of lavender, their eyes locked, floating across, and dodging people as she came closer, ever so close. Jack opened his arms, waiting. Jack puckered his lips. Sarah was inches away and then inches to the right of him, and now inches behind him, and feet... *And what's goin' on?*

Sarah ran into Gene's arms and planted a big, long kiss. Gene's glasses steamed up and condensed to the point of needing windshield wipers. Gene slowly fell backward and hit the ground. Shaking his head, Jack brushed it off and, unlike a week before, ran to Gene's rescue with water, along with Edgar.

Chapter 29
Gold Rush?

Three days later, the Bandits took a trip to Times Square to make their *Good Morning America* debut and tell their story about fending off two of America's Most Wanted. Jack enjoyed every moment of the limelight, while Gene and Edgar enjoyed a free vacation, stopping by and checking out the many sites. Their time was a blast until it ended sooner than they hoped. While on the Empire State Building tour, Jack's sense of adventure wasn't well-received.

"Guys," Jack said enthusiastically to Gene and Edgar. "Let's pee off the top of the building!"

Gene shook his head and glanced at Edgar before security abruptly ended their tour.

In other news, later that week, when they got back to Boonetown, Edgar's brother was sentenced to serve six months in jail for manufacturing and trafficking illegal candy contraband. Edgar stayed with Jack's family for the time being, but his dad promised to see him more often than before. Edgar was happy about that and made plans to spend many weekends with his dad.

Jack, Edgar, and Gene watched the report live from Gene's screened-in porch that afternoon.

"Whoa, Edgar," Jack said. "Your brother made the news! Just like us. We're all famous!" Jack smiled while Edgar and Gene giggled along, shoving popcorn into their mouths.

"Jack, look!" Gene said, pointing to the screen. "It's the emaciated, crazy reporter who interviewed you."

"We have a Great Gauley Gold Rush goin' on here," Joan Morgan, the reporter, said.

"Yeah," Jack said. "She's like demented and doesn't know it!"

"There has been priceless gold found in the Gauley River, and prospectors from all around the country are flocking into Boonetown. I mean, flocking! Some are calling it the greatest gold rush since the forty-niners in 1849. The rush is real. Historians say the precious gold found in banks of the Gauley may hold over a billion dollars in value. Some even say the Ark of the Covenant is in these grounds. Billionaire businessmen are even putting offers to buy the land around the Gauley to get the best gold. One billionaire wants to buy the land and rename the town Boomtown. The proposal is to down all the trees surrounding the river and possibly suck the water out of the river. He deems the trees and water a hindrance to finding the riches. Local conservation movements are saying no. I'm saying, bring on more news! Joan Morgan, live from Channel Six, Boonetown."

Click. Jack turned off the television as he, Edgar, and Gene laughed at the news and walked toward the door.

Edgar carried a chest, and Jack and Gene, shovels. They headed toward the field to bury a new treasure for someone else to find.

Gene's mom called for him before he left. Gene looked at Jack and Edgar. "Hey, I'll meet you guys outside in a few minutes. My mom wants to talk." As they waited outside, Jack and Edgar noticed a couple and their newborn pull up in Gene's driveway, alongside a lady in a realty car.

Jack looked at Edgar. "Um, what's going on?"

Edgar shrugged his shoulders. "Um, n-not sure. S-Selling, m-maybe?"

Gene busted out the door, and briskly walked toward them. He greeted them with red eyes.

"Let's go," Gene said, as he walked past Jack and Edgar toward the field. Jack and Edgar jogged to keep up before they stopped in the field.

"Are you moving?" Jack asked Gene, with a frail twinge in his voice.

Gene looked at the ground, and then looked at Jack and Edgar, nodding. "Yep." Gene cried as Jack and Edgar consoled him. Gene composed himself and said, "My mom got a new job, and it's out of state. It sucks. She starts in like a week."

"Really? Where are you going to live then, with the new people moving in? In our treehouse?" Jack asked.

"Um…" Gene looked at Jack, tears mixed with a laugh. "I'm going to move with them, stupid! Duh." Gene's shoulders slumped.

"Wow!" Jack's eyes welled up and his lips moved. "I'm…" Jack's head nodded. "I'm really, really gonna miss you."

"M-Me, too," Edgar said.

"Yeah," Gene said. "But we can still hang out together and play video games, you know."

The three walked deeper into the field, the place where Jack and Gene spent their whole childhoods, their whole lives playing. Every memory was created there, and the only world they knew would be shared for one last time.

They walked into the field to bury a chest for someone else to find, enjoy, and share in a great adventure, years down the road. Jack wrapped his arm around Gene's shoulders, and Edgar joined in on the other side, as they walked toward Spangler's.

"Well, I'm sure you'll come back a bunch. And when you come back, I'm going to have a huge jump, and one of those tightropes like Lito had," Jack said.

In the field between the jumps, the evergreens, and Spangler's Creek, a bridge between childhood and adulthood was formed. A bridge that no flood could ever wash away. Jack planted a shovel into the ground and dug a hole big enough for the chest.

"Gene, can you do the honors?" Jack asked. "Make that trumpet noise with your mouth and elbow, if you could?" Jack smiled.

"All right, one last time." Gene smiled. "Ba bum bum bum ba ba bum bum bumm!"

The three placed the chest in the ground. Gene put the map to the treasure inside, along with their own letter:

Dear Whomever,

Congrats on finding this chest. Underneath is a map, which will lead you to a treasure of great riches. Be careful, however, as there is crazy whitewater, and you'll definitely need a floatation device. Also, be aware of a crazy snake which may be dead by the time you read this, but its descendants are probably going to be crazy, too. It seems to happen that way with many living species. Please, bring a friend, and know that the adventure is the true treasure.

Good luck,
Boonetown Bandits

P.S. "Find what you want, dream and believe, and take one step at a time toward it. And soon that dream will become reality." —Lito and the Bandits (with a little inspiration from google)

Jack wrote his own quotes with a different alias:

"Live your life, have fun, find friends, and meet good people along the way. Long live Jack Mathias!"
"Sometimes, like pizza, the best things in life are a little cheesy!"

"If you search long enough, you may find a hidden treasure, buried deep inside of the person in the mirror."
—Ben Dover.

They placed the letter in the box, latched it, and buried it in the ground.

***

A few days later, Jack walked to the U-Haul van in Gene's driveway. Gene's mom hugged Jack before Jack saw Gene in the back seat.

"See ya, my brother from another mother," Gene said, putting out his knuckles as their fists met and exploded.

Jack smiled. "I'm gonna take you out in Warhammer tomorrow. What time should I get on?"

"I'll be on at seven, but I'll just text you a few minutes before," Gene said.

"All right, sounds good!"

The van pulled out of the driveway.

"Bye," Jack said under his breath. He stood frozen like a statue with his hand in the air.

Jack's last view of Gene in person that summer was the back of his head, with the taillights fading down the road. The same road they routinely walked home from the school bus and the same asphalt that gave them both their first scar. But for Jack, the scar on this day hurt a little bit more than the others before.

On a happier note, Jack and Edgar's friendship blossomed, and they spent the rest of the summer together. Edgar took the place of Gene as Jack's new best friend. But they still kept in touch with Gene via FaceTime and gaming. In other news, after weeks of intensive searching, Lito's body was never found. Jack believed he escaped the rapids and headed northeast up the Appalachians. Others say if you see a mist on the Gauley River, it's Lito's spirit watching over. Regardless of who you believe, it was a summer the Boonetown Bandits will never forget. And the memory will stick with them forever.

Epilogue:
Revenge?

In an undisclosed, dim-lit room, five men sat, wearing fancy business suits and staring across a long, high-glossed wooden table at the back of a high diamond-and-gold-plated chair. Swiveling around, the man in the chair—older with gray hair—sported a black leisure suit with red, matching pocket hankies. His face was weathered but calm. His thick, wrinkly fingers tapped the arms of the chair, as he rolled the gold band on his pinkie like a hula hoop in gym class. His lips slowly opened. The men stared intently at his mouth.

"Who is this, ah, Jack Mathias and these… Boonetown Bandits?" the man known as Papi asked, scoffing with a thick Brooklyn accent. "I think he picked on the a-wrong guys. I want you to find these characters. Capeesh?"

Coming Soon!

**Jack Mathias and the
Boonetown Bandits:
Camp, Oh No!**